I0689388

The Morals of St. Sadie

by Alan Greenwell

**A novel about art,
the funding of education in Africa
and about morality.**

Sadie thought she was so upright
but found herself slipping into a
world where deceit, theft and worse
seemed unavoidable.

Later, marooned on another
continent, she reflects on how her
downfall came about and on how to
redeem herself.

The Morals of St. Sadie

Main Characters

Sadie Brown
Walter Alexander, her maternal Grandfather

Mel, Sadie's best friend
Kyle, Mel's brother

Jill Carruthers
Julius, Jill's father
Tariq, her partner
Harry, her son
Baz, her half brother

Sean Smith

Marion, charity worker
Joseph, Head teacher
Augusta, Joseph's wife
Suzan and Olivette, Joseph's pupils

1

Deceit, theft then murder, -- but all trying to make the world a better place. How could I have ever believed this? At first I blamed my Grandfather for my problems, but that's unfair. He was pursuing his own passions. It's me who was at fault. At twenty three, I was young and easily swayed. I know that now. I used to think I was so good – morally that is. My best friend Mel would have stopped me, but I hardly told her anything. I was an idiot. Now I am marooned on another continent, asking myself if I will ever see Mel or my Grandfather again.

As I write, four years after the events, I ask myself why I didn't stop myself sliding deeper and deeper. Each step down seemed acceptable. Add them all together and you have me now, appalled by myself and marooned far from my homeland. I've decided to write this all down as an act of contrition. I'm writing it for my children, if I ever have any. I can't let them read it all. And it's not to be read until they are mature. I hope they reach that state sooner than I did.

My Grandfather is still alive -- and we're thousands of miles apart. We manage an occasional email – and that's it. I can't yet explain to him why I have to stay in Africa. He knows a bit but I cannot burden him with everything. I say I'm involved with someone here, which is true, but far from the whole truth. I feel torn apart, living so far from my family and my closest friends. But I cannot go back to Britain, not yet.

I'll start off with the job, my first after college -- as a temp in the Gallery Elite. I thought it was marvellous, but in reality there was little to do. Sitting at the reception desk looking down the gallery past the paintings, towards the door, hoping someone would come in. My boss Jill was working in the office through the glass window behind me, when she was in. It was my second week and I was probably daydreaming about Kyle again -- stupid because even then I knew he was not for me. Then someone forced the gallery door open far too hard and almost fell in. A visitor, at last.

This portly middle-aged hippy was not the gallery type. He wrenched the door back on its hinges, then made a running waddle the length of the gallery towards me. In his red top, jeans and large tinted specs, he steamed up, brandishing a newspaper.

Bald and sweating, he barked out, 'Who the hell are you?'

I stuttered out, 'Sadie -- Sadie Brown.' I looked over my shoulder to check that Jill really was in the office, then took a grip.

'What exactly can I do for you?'

'Damn all, by the sound of you. I bloody well own this place, don't I?' I caught the East End accent. 'And I don't like your uppity manners, miss. Now where the hell is Jill?'

I felt myself go crimson and then, thank God, heard Jill clip-clopping up behind me.

'Pop - what's happened? Here - come into the office. It's OK Sadie - just hold the fort.'

As they entered the office, I heard, 'What the hell is going on, Pop? You frightened that girl...'

'You just wait till you see this....' And the office door was slammed shut.

I sat down again at my desk and told myself to calm down. That angry little man? Jill's father? Owns this gallery?

I had found it difficult to place 'Gallery Elite' among the private London galleries. It was small, only twenty five paintings placed along either side of a long white room with an obliquely angled ceiling, giving a pleasantly lop-sided feel to the place. The current exhibition was split between two artists – the high walled side was hung with sombre abstracted heads, which I liked. Close up heads filling large canvases, big features especially the eyes. The low walled side had loud swirling demented acrylics, mostly red, dramatic and exciting -- all blood and madness. The gallery was poorly placed and the marketing was weak. The web site was too like a games advert, with distracting graphic devices going off all over the place and absolutely no sense of audience. But Jill had selected the two artists and as far as I knew, she edited the web site. Why should I complain if it funded my job? Except, as my best friend Mel kept telling me, with few sales it couldn't last long.

I could hear raised voices from the office and hoped it was nothing to do with my 'uppity manners'. I was only the temporary receptionist. I can talk street if necessary, but surely in an art gallery, you have to adopt a suitable manner? That sounds like I was a snob.

About twenty minutes later, Jill and her father emerged from the office, him in a calmer state.

Almost jovially, he turned to his daughter.

'Jill, hadn't you better introduce me to this young lady?'

Jill rolled her eyes, 'It's alright Sadie -- he's

working his way round to an apology. This is Julius, my father. Pop, meet our new receptionist Sadie. She's an Art History graduate, so watch what you say.'

As we shook hands, Julius Carruthers looked deep into my eyes. 'Sadie – I like that name. Look, sorry I was rude. Normally I'm calm as a lamb.'

Jill laughed. 'Ten percent of the time – on the good days.'

There in his chubby face were Jill's blue-green eyes -- and his smile radiated his daughter's confident charm. When he finally released my hand, I noticed the same trick as Jill of holding out his hands as he spoke, as if he was about to embrace me. I stepped back but he came forward, slightly too close for my liking.

'And by the way, you've got a lovely speaking manner - brings a bit of class into the place.'

'That's alright then. My dad has a short fuse.'

They waited for me to make my peace. I was still unsure so I paused before I came out with, 'Right. I suppose it's all good training for facing the public.'

Julius guffawed, 'Wow - that's the first time my temper's been called training. What do they call it? - staff development.' His voice rose, 'Good God - they'll be hiring me out for courses next. I'll have a whole new career!'

'Calm down Pop -- we've got to go now. Are you happy locking up, Sadie?'

'Of course.'

'And opening tomorrow at eleven?'

'Yes. That's fine….er, nice to meet you Mr Carruthers.'

'It's Julius - and great to meet you Sadie. I mean it.'

As they set off, Jill turned and said, 'Oh and

Sadie, I might not be in tomorrow, not sure yet. You'll manage OK, won't you?'

I thought -- good, she trusts me.

I watched them walking away. Jill was warm, confident, strong -- and I quite liked her loud trouser suits. They worked with her bouncy style, made her look not too overweight. But some years on and without the high heels, I thought she would begin to look like her father. For now, their heads were tilted towards each other, focused on something. They obviously were close, which was nice, though his swing from enraged to gushing left me uneasy. However he was Jill's dad; that was a plus, surely?

Since my mother's death seven years ago, I was often looking for new role models and Jill just slotted in. I was beginning to not just admire her, but to put her on a pedestal. That was a danger that I only understood later. I thought to myself, in ten or fifteen years I want to be like her. But at that stage I knew almost nothing about her.

I had a few minutes before closing time so I went back to the receptionist's desk -- and a bit more dreamtime. Jill had deliberately set out to repair the hurt her father had caused - and she trusted me with the keys. I felt happy. The young Sadie, the 23-year-old me, was so easily pleased.

After a while, I started running through the locking up procedure, then I went into the office where the security system was housed. On the desk was a large map of some foreign coastal area - and a brochure titled 'ARW -- Africa Read Write - Education for Girls' - with notes scribbled in the margins. I knew that Jill was involved in this -- and it interested me. I'd been to South Africa in my gap year, visiting some relatives and had seen that education for girls was vitally important.

Julius had left his newspaper. The headlines were, "ART LOVER SHOT". A London man had been kneecapped in his home by a masked stranger and was now hospitalised. Nothing was stolen. Was this why Jill's father had been upset? Perhaps the shot man was a friend -- or perhaps he feared for himself?

Locking up, I thought -- my second week and she trusts me. I decided to have a quick coffee in the flat that Mel and I shared, then to call on Walter, my Grandfather. He had helped me financially through my degree and was keen on art himself, He was absurdly pleased about my new job. If he had known about the lack of visitors to Gallery Elite, he would have been less impressed.

An hour later I let myself into Walter's front door.

When my mother was killed in a road accident, Walter and Marie, my maternal grandparents, had adopted me. Not legally, just emotionally. They seemed to need a daughter and I was ready to fill the breach. I was sixteen when my mother died and my grandmother was still alive then. She died of a stroke soon after and that was when I started getting closer to Walter. I was studying in Bristol but I came and stayed with him in London during the holidays. He was still able to get out to galleries and films then. He owned some property and when he knew I was after a gallery job in London, he loaned me this flat, rent-free, not so far from where he lived. So I felt amazingly lucky to both find this job near him and have a flat with a spare bedroom for my best friend Mel. I was able to see more of Walter. Most weeks I spent at least one evening with him. His heart condition meant that we stayed in. We had a snack, talked, watched some TV or a DVD about art.

'Sold anything today?' He always asked that.

'No, but I met the owner, Jill's dad.'

'Oh. And what did you make of him?'

'A middle aged thug, except that he's Jill's father, so he can't be. He seemed like two different people.'

'Odd -- he's the owner, she runs it, sells nothing and employs you. So what's his game? Is it a plaything for his daughter?'

Walter had been a banker. I was still bruised by that 'uppity' comment and didn't want to know that there was any 'game' going on.

'The two of them get on well. It must be the sort of thing that caring parents and grandparents do for their younger relatives. Like you and me. I'd never have been able to afford uni otherwise -- or a London flat.'

'Get away with you. Your father would have got something together if I hadn't been around.'

'Maybe.'

I doubted that as my doctor father buried himself in his work when my mother died. Then he married a colleague who was impossible. The two of them flitted to New Zealand, with my little brother Will, with barely a word to me. Anyway, at seventeen, I was much happier living with Walter and Marie in London, than with a stupid stepmother on the far side of the world.

I heated the food that Walter's housekeeper had left, then we watched a couple of art programmes on TV. He got quite excited because one of these mentioned Francis Bacon. This was an interest we didn't share. He had met Bacon when he was younger and was fascinated by his paintings. I thought they were brilliant but sick. We had watched a film biography of Bacon a few weeks earlier. I know that people of genius are often troubled, but this man seemed vicious. However out of respect for my Grandfather, I held back on my dislike of the dead painter.

His fascination for Bacon's paintings made me look at Walter afresh. I'm no painter but I quite wanted to do some portrait photos of him. Walter had quite a sensual face, long with thick lips. Probably dangerously good-looking when he was young. I don't know much about his marriage but guess he must have had a colourful life at some stage before settling into a respectable marriage (as far as I knew) and then making money.

2

Next morning, only my second week in Gallery Elite. I was getting used to everything -- opening up, security, lights -- nothing demanding, but it was responsibility.

Why so few visitors? They needed better publicity, a better web site. My head was buzzing with possibilities, but Jill might resent a pushy temp. With little to do but surf the web, I could at least explore some ideas, then discreetly, at the right time, present them to Jill -- and try to edge my way towards being indispensable.

After a few minutes, the office phone rang, 'Hi -- it's Paul from New Art Plus here. Is Jill around?' He sounded cheery -- and slightly familiar.

'Sorry Paul, she's not here...'

'So who is this?'

'Sadie -- I'm on reception...'

'Of course. Jill mentioned you were coming....'

This surprised me. 'Oh, right. So is there any message?'

'It's OK -- I'll catch up with her soon. Bye.'

I left a note for Jill about the call.

An hour later, a visitor arrived -- at last. An attractive man in his early thirties swept in like a dancer -- muscular, confident. He ignored the paintings, smiled slightly and held my eyes as he approached. He offered his hand, 'Hi. Good to meet you Sadie.'

He had a shaven head with a goatee, and rather striking features

I was sure I recognised his accent, 'Hi -- you're Paul aren't you?'

'Who's Paul? No -- I'm Sean.'

'Right. Sorry. So how do you know my name?'

He was very presentable, this Sean -- wide mouth, cropped blond hair and striking eyes, dark blue with a hint of violet, unusual face – slightly asymmetrical. He seemed to be charged with energy, as if he might do a somersault any time.

'Can't you guess?' I gave a half-smile and held his eyes.

He cocked his head and almost whispered, 'Jill told me all about you.' Was he teasing? Or flirting?

I mimicked his gesture and whispered back, 'Well sorry but I don't think she mentioned you at all.... '

'That fits. I'm just a menial. I work with Julius. Have you met Jill's old man yet? On projects. Seen the web site?'

'Yes....you do the web site?'

'Sure -- you like it?'

'It's striking. Really clever.' I was being kind, for clever was all it was. It was not targeted on any market I could spot.

'That's the aim -- I'm quite pleased with it. Where's Jill? Not in yet?'

He peered through the frosted glass of the office, then made towards the office door. I was a little taken aback and followed him, but he seemed to know what he was doing.

'Not today. Was she expecting you?'

He went straight over to the filing cabinet.

'I'm sure we said today -- she must have got mixed up. I need some stuff -- bottom drawer I think

-- blast, it's locked.'

I thought -- would Jill approve? But we're all colleagues....

'Don't worry -- the key's under here but don't tell anyone...'

'Great -- you're a star Sadie -- .'

I thought of us two, I'm not the star. He was soon bending down and flicking through the folders -- quite a fetching sight, actually.

'Jill's well organised -- but there's loads of her Africa rubbish in here -- ah now, this could be it, yes, here we are. I just want this guy's contact details.... can I use the copier?'

That was all he wanted, a copy of one sheet of A4. Quickly sorted. Key back in place -- and he was moving towards the door.

'Great to meet you Sadie. There's no need to mention to Jill that I've been -- I want to surprise her.'

'OK. Well, perhaps see you again one day. By the way, where do you work -- I mean on the web?'

'From my flat mostly. Why?...'

'I've always wanted to learn more about it...'

'I'll show you one day. It's not that exciting. I'd invite you round sometime. I'm a bit busy right now but soon....why not?'

I didn't want to seem too eager but couldn't resist saying, 'Right. That would be great.'

He left as rapidly as he came, with speed and grace. Just walking out, he looked so lithe, almost beautiful. I realised later that I was being played for an innocent and had no idea at all what he was up to. Jill had never heard of Paul of New Art Plus, who rang before Sean arrived and I didn't think to connect them until much later. I didn't mention Sean's visit to her. I should have.

When I got home to the flat, Mel's brother Kyle was there. Mel was my closest friend at college. She was always the clever one; she knew there's no money to be made in Art so changed courses after our first year, then went into retail management -- and got promoted every few months. Away from work she spent time with her boyfriend Justin who lived with his parents. I was waiting for him to ask if he could move in with Mel, but this was my flat (Walter's really), and it would have been a squeeze. I thought Mel felt guilty about seeing less of me, with her work and boyfriend -- and that made her nudge me in the direction of Kyle, her brother.

Kyle came to the flat for an evening most weeks, and occasionally slept on the sofa. He was a year younger than Mel and me, skinny, funny and friendly. An actor – at least he'd done a drama course but he mostly worked in a bar not far from my gallery. He was different from how I expected an actor to be -- quite modest and with his sister's good nature. He had good features, a lively and malleable face and tended to quiz me quite closely about what I was up to, even what I was thinking about; I enjoyed this but was often disappointed by his reactions to my acute observations. Anyway Kyle and I hit it off; he was keen on me. I held back from getting too serious beyond an occasional cuddle and sometimes more, when Mel was out. I always made it clear that we were just having some fun, that we weren't in a serious relationship -- and he seemed to accept that, but then he wasn't a subtle person.

At college I had some relationships that mostly ended painfully and too soon, so I'd learned to be cautious. If that pattern repeated with Kyle, where would that leave me and Mel?

Mel and I got on so well; I couldn't risk Kyle getting between us. In any case, according to his sister, Kyle might be seeing someone else. Kyle talked as if he just rented a room in a friend's house but he and this friend had rows, then he would spend time with us. If you pressed him, he wouldn't say much -- and it wasn't my business. Anyway he was nice to have around -- and I suppose he was the nearest thing I had to a boyfriend at that point in my life.

That particular night, Mel's boyfriend was working, so Mel and Kyle suggested a takeaway and a DVD, which suited me.

Once we settled down over our pizzas, Kyle started gently quizzing me - his usual ploy.

'So did you have a good day today? Any visitors?'

'Better than usual. And I met a new colleague.'

I thought again about what Sean had said about not letting Jill know about his visit. But Mel and Kyle weren't Jill, so no issue.

Mel said, 'Oh? We've had Jill and Jill's horrible dad, so who was this? Another relative?'

'No, a youngish guy who does the website.'

Kyle ducked down a bit over his plate and stayed silent. It was much later that I understood this slightly odd behaviour.

'Didn't you say the gallery website was crap?'

'Well yes, It's clever -- loads of flashy gimmicks. The guy's a wiz but he's got no idea at all about targeting the art market. For a start it has to be a work of art in itself and the only work of art this guy's interested in is himself.'

Kyle kept his head well down on his pizza.

'Really? Tell us more. Is he a work of art?'

'He is rather. Fit looking and quite striking. More your sort than mine.'

'Well thanks, but I've got Justin, haven't I? You're the one I worry about.'

I said nothing but wondered if she was thinking about Kyle and me again. She'd sometimes said the four of us ought to go out together.

'Will you see much of him? This - what's he called?'

'Sean. He said he's going to show me how he does the web pages. I can handle Dreamweaver but I should think that's beneath Sean.'

Kyle turned to me and said slightly aggressively, 'Are you having the rest of your pizza or shall I grab it?'

I stared at him. So did his sister. He backed down. 'Sorry -- I was just...I'm a bit hungry. Anyway, what are we watching tonight?'

And the tension dissolved, but that conversation came back to me later. At that point I didn't understand what Kyle had got himself into, nor that I was going to be following him.

3

On arrival at work next day, I was surprised to find the gallery door unlocked and the lights on. The paintings were quite subtly lit. As you enter, the sub-Freud portraits are on the right -- the garish red splurges on the left. I always looked at the portraits when I entered the gallery and I was beginning to like them more. They were mostly extreme close-ups of not very beautiful people, slightly oblique face views, with large eyes staring out of the canvas. They weren't photographic but emphasized the geometry of the head. I don't think the subjects would be flattered.

As I neared the reception desk, a head peered at me through the office window. It was Jill who gave a great wave -- or was it just a wave? -- me ever hopeful.

In the office, she was sitting over that same map and some other papers.

'Hi Sadie! Great timing - I'm desperate for a coffee.'

'Shall I fix you one.'

'Would you? And have one yourself -- there's some chocky biscuits over there. I need to get away from this stuff for a bit. It's driving me crazy.'

'What is it you're doing? I don't recognize that map.....'

'That's no surprise. It's northern Kembazi.'

'That's in Africa, isn't it?'

'West Africa. I'm working on a project there - girls' education, trying to give them a different life from marrying at fifteen -- or younger -- and having loads of kids.'

'But they're only kids themselves…'

'Sadie, if you were there, you'd have five or six kids of your own to look after by now…'

I was horrified. 'Really -- I'd never cope. So what is it you do -- in the project?'

'We raise funds to pay for school fees -- and try to build new schools.'

'Wow. That's fantastic.'

'It's very practical. I've been out there a couple of times.'

'That must have been fascinating. I'd love to help with something like that.'

'Oh, you are. Really. You're freeing me up to work on it.'

I started getting the coffees and from where I was standing, I could see along the gallery.

'There's someone coming -- we've got a visitor. I'll go and see if they need anything....'

Surprise, surprise -- a small boy, perhaps four or five years old, was standing inside the gallery door, staring along the gallery at me. He was mixed-race and his hair was closely cropped, blue shirt and grey jeans. I smiled at him and was about to step forward when I felt Jill leaning on me, peering over my shoulder. Suddenly the boy lurched forward.

'Mummy -- Mummy...'

He ran the length of the gallery, sidestepped me and threw himself into Jill's arms. She lifted him up and embraced him closely.

'You brave boy -- you've got here all by yourself. You're so clever!'

He was panting slightly from the run.

'Daddy brought me to the door.'

'Oh, I see.'

'He opened the door. It's too hard for me...'

Jill placed him back on the floor. 'Right -- now Harry, I want you to meet Sadie. Sadie works here with me.'

Harry looked closely up into my face with large brown eyes. I melted.

'This is my son, Harry. Do you two want to shake hands?.'

We shook hands rather seriously, then Jill herded us into the office. Harry sat on his mother's lap. Prompted by Jill, while I fixed the coffee, Harry told me what he had done today, in great detail. I was taken with this little charmer, and by the emerging picture of Jill's world. After a few minutes, Harry was sitting with crayons and paper at the end of the desk, to draw us a picture.

Jill turned to me. 'While I've still got you, you must tell me more about your Grandfather. What sort of things does he like?'

I'd mentioned Walter during the interview for the temp post, to show that I knew something about the 'private art collector'. But my heart sank at the 'while I've still got you.'

'Modern stuff -- mainly British. He's got quite a good small collection.'

'Is he still buying?'

'Yes. He's more or less housebound now but he still buys occasionally. He met Francis Bacon -- that's his claim to fame...'

'Really -- I'm impressed. A friend of Bacon -- wow. Do you think I could meet him, your Grandfather? Would he be interested?'

At this point I should have asked myself why? I saw it as an interest in me, a gesture of friendship.

Silly me!

'I should think so. I can always ask him.'

'That would be great. Let's see if we can combine a little business with pleasure. Now, how is the young artist doing? Harry -- can we see please?'

He held it up, two balloon-like figures, and said, 'It's not finished yet'.

I knew enough about children to say, 'That's brilliant.'

Harry jumped up and ran to the door. He'd heard something.

I looked up to see a young black man loping down the gallery towards us. Slender, stylish in red top and jeans. Very black with close cropped hair.

As he entered the office, Jill spoke quite sharply. 'At last. I was getting worried.'

'Sorry love. They'd run out. He'll have to make do with what we've got.'

'Well he won't like that....'

To me she said, 'Harry's very fussy about his food -- drives us mad. This is Tariq, my other half. Tariq, I told you about Sadie, our new receptionist, standing in for Meg.'

I was taken by this impressive 'other half' -- and tried to stop staring. We shook hands rather formally.

'You two might be working together now and then, so it's good you've met. And Sadie's met Julius. He was in a state...'

Tariq hesitated then said, 'Well I hope you can manage Julius's states better than I can.'

I caught his glance as he looked down and thought I saw someone slightly ill at ease, perhaps shy.

'To be honest, I didn't know how to react -- but he apologised afterwards...'

'That's my father -- kick everyone in sight then pour gallons of oil. Now we have to move and feed Master Harry...'

As Tariq lifted up his son, and admired his drawing, I asked him, 'So where are you based, Tariq?'

'Me? Oh, now you're asking...mainly with this young man.' He spoke with a slight northern accent and later Jill told he was brought up in Leeds.

He shrugged a little and looked at Jill who said, 'We share the parenting so I can manage the business with my father -- and deal with the Africa project. That takes loads of time.'

Turning to Tariq, she added, 'And then you do various bits and bobs for Julius yourself, don't you?'

'Sure. Moving paintings around, stuff like that. Mostly I'm looking after Master Harry, aren't I?'

I said rather too enthusiastically, 'Sounds good. You're both lucky. I mean all three of you.'

They both laughed at this.

After they had left, I mulled over this small family. I had never met anyone like Jill - and now to learn of her brilliant African venture. And sweet little Harry -- perhaps I could baby-sit sometime? Tariq -- I was really struck by his -- not exactly beauty but...style? But why was he shy, almost sheepish? I thought, I'll have to get to know him better -- part of the Jill venture, as I found myself calling it.

Then I told myself to stop being stupid. Jill had made it clear that I was only filling in for Meg -- and Tariq was her 'other half'.

4

My luck was in. The following Monday Jill was panicking over her babysitter falling ill.

'It's a thank you meal to our Africa donors. Some of them give hundreds every year. It's really important to tell them what we're doing with the money.'

'When is it?'

'This Wednesday...'

'Well I'll do it Jill. If you'll have me. I mean I'm free but would Harry be alright with me?'

'Would you? Oh you angel. Harry'll be fine. He loves you. He wouldn't stop chattering about you the other day.'

'Really?'

'You admired his drawing; that does it for Harry.'

So it was fixed.

The idea of babysitting for Jill and Tariq was quite exciting. I was to arrive early to look after Harry as his parents got ready. Tariq was fixing up a slide show of the school developments in Africa -- and Marion, the Africa-Read-Write administrator, was joining them. When I arrived at their ground-floor flat, Jill opened the door and Harry rushed up to me and hugged my legs. He was already in his pyjamas. The plan was for me to read a last story to him in bed as he nodded off. Jill was in a dramatic, tight scarlet dress. Tariq was still in jeans and T-shirt, watching the TV news.

The flat was large, colourful and messy. Harry immediately took my hand and dragged me over to help him finish a jigsaw. I had to work my way among his books, crayons, toys, which were scattered all around.

'Just ignore the mess, Sadie. It's all Harry's stuff and he doesn't do tidiness yet. And this isn't one of our cleaning days.'

Tariq was tetchy. 'I was feeding him, so I couldn't tidy up as well. Anyway, Sadie doesn't mind - do you?'

I shook my head. Harry prodded me to attend to the jigsaw.

'That's alright darling. You fed Harry -- and that was a great help.'

To me, she said, 'I had some urgent Africa emails to finish....before Marion comes.'

Tariq was not placated. 'God! An evening with Marion. I don't know how you stand the woman...'

'I know, I know -- she's difficult -- but just for this one evening. You don't have to sit beside her.'

She turned to me, 'Marion's our administrator -- and she's marvellous in her way, but a little trying. She's coming here for a lift. It's a thank you meal for donors. All rather spartan. Obviously we can't splash out too much. How are you two getting on down there? Are you nearly finished Harry? It's late....'

Harry ignored her so I said, 'Only six more pieces to go...'

Tariq said, 'I think I'll be ill this evening -- that'll be my excuse -- I'll stay in with Sadie.'

I felt myself blush and lowered my head. I knew he wasn't being serious. Jill murmured something for Tariq's ears only.

Tariq snapped at her. 'No -- and I don't need reminding. It's sorted.'

The doorbell rang. Jill jumped. 'That'll be Marion. Tariq darling, please get changed -- or we'll never get away!'

As Tariq slouched out, Jill turned to me. 'Sadie,

can you be a dear and chat with Marion, while I get my things together?' She added in a low voice, 'Tariq's not very well. He hasn't taken his pills today so that he can have a drink.'

So perhaps Tariq was not the perfect partner after all, but someone to be managed? However my focus was on the Africa project, and the need to engage with this Marion person. I prepared to stand, but Harry held me down and we ended up laughing and rolling around on the floor.

Jill was gushing at the door. 'Marion -- welcome! We're almost ready. Tariq's just changing.'

'I hope he won't be long.' She sounded deep voiced and bossy. 'We really need to be there before our guests -- that's only courteous.'

'This is Sadie -- over there with Harry. Come on you two. Say hello to Marion...'

I was standing up by now. Harry was climbing up me so I was forced to lift him and walked towards Marion holding the little boy. She was a tall well-built woman, in her early fifties with an air of rumpled respectability. Her face was large and flat. She wore a cream top and skirt and a long open coat. The square glasses and the thin wide mouth were not appealing. But as my Grandfather often said, you don't need to be a beauty to have a life of value.

'Sadie works with me in the gallery. She's looking after Harry tonight.'

'I see. How do you do, Sadie. And this must be your son?'

I said, 'Hello. Jill's son actually.'

Marion glared at me. 'I think I knew that.'

'Sorry – my silly joke. Jill, why don't you get ready and we'll.....have a chat.'

'Oh thanks. Is that alright Marion? We won't be

long...'

Jill left us, presumably to chivvy Tariq. Marion looked at her watch.

After a few awkward moments, I came out with, 'I'm very interested in your work in Africa -- in fact I'd love to help.'

'We need more volunteers so I'm pleased to hear it.' Her tone said -- and so you ought!

Harry wanted Marion's attention. 'My name's Harry...'

'Really -- is it? I think I know someone else called Harry.'

'I don't know anyone. Just me. Do you want to see my jigsaw?'

'I'm afraid we don't have time for that tonight.' Harry's face crumpled. 'Well, I suppose I can. Yes, alright -- if you're quick.'

I carried Harry over to the jigsaw and observed Marion's attempt to show an interest.

After a while, Harry said, 'Do you want a go? I can mess it up for you...'

Marion froze, then Jill rushed in. 'Sorry about that...we're ready at last.' She was followed by Tariq looking rather splendid in a dark suit. Marion and he nodded to each other – no warmth there.

Marion leant towards Harry and said in a public whisper, 'Sorry I can't do your jigsaw. I'm going out with your parents and we're already very late...'

After parental kisses goodnight to Harry, the three left. He was content to be carried to his bedroom, tucked into bed and read to, until he nodded off.

I settled down on a cosy sofa, with some snacks and wine that had been set out for me -- and reflected on the evening. Harry was fun and yes, I was keen to help with the Africa Read Write project. Could I stand much of Marion? Yes, I could cope. And what's up with Tariq?

At around eleven, Jill and Tariq returned. They sat down with me, tired but apparently satisfied with the event.

'There's plenty wine left -- I've only had a couple of glasses...'

Jill quickly said, 'No thanks, we've both had enough.'

Tariq looked red-eyed and sleepy. 'I'll have a glass....'

I poured him one and asked, 'Did it all go alright?'

'Yes it was fine. We got through it anyway.'

Tariq said, 'And after all that fuss about being late, we were the first there...'

Picking up the cue, I asked if Marion enjoyed herself and that started Tariq off.

'Marion never enjoys herself -- and nobody enjoys Marion -- that's the truth. She hates men...'

'Oh Tariq, of course she doesn't. She's just not very good with people. But she drives the project forwards. We need her. She keeps everyone on target.'

'Yes, everyone's got to keep to her targets -- and she's obsessed with time. As if life's not challenging enough without Marion and her bloody targets.'

'Now darling, she was genuinely grateful for you setting up her slide show.'

'She said she was, made a great show of it to the visitors, but when we were getting ready, the endless fussing drove me mad. I'm not her skivvy! I'd better have another drink.'

I lent forward to lift the wine bottle but Jill came in quickly. 'No, no more darling, please. Look, I promise I'll keep Marion away from you in future. Is that a bargain?'

Tariq looked at me, at the wine bottle, then at Jill. 'Alright. I'm jiggered anyway.'

He got up and turned to me. 'Sadie, I don't mean to be anti-social but I'm off to my bed. Thank you for looking after Harry -- and well, just for being here...'. And he left, unsteadily.

I thought I ought to leave, but Jill came across to the sofa to sit closer to me...

'Tariq's drunk too much tonight. He'll suffer in the morning -- and so will I.'

'Oh. I'm sorry...'

'He's on medication. When he misses the pills, it makes him low the next day. It's rather difficult.'

'It must be, for both of you. Is he -- a bit depressed?'

'Yes, a depressive illness. Is it that obvious?'

'No, not at all, but I've got an aunt who had it. My mother's sister...'

'Oh. How long was she ill?'

'About six months -- and then it was over...'

I couldn't tell her that it ended in suicide.

'This has just started, so it sounds like we've got a bit to go yet. Anyway I wanted to talk with you Sadie because I need your help. Tariq won't accept his -- condition -- so I have to plan around it. It means some days he can't work. Tomorrow's going to be one of those days but there's not much on right now so that's fine. But when we hit a busy period, I'll need extra help from someone I can trust....'

'Well, I'll do anything I can Jill....'

'That's wonderful. I'd only ask you to do stuff you're happy with – and feel competent to do. That sounds a bit patronising but we've got to be realistic. I mean there's various things that Tariq does that I couldn't ask you to do -- moving heavy paintings around -- but I can shuffle the tasks among the team. And often it only means having you at the end of a phone, as a standby.'

'OK -- that sounds alright.'

'Actually I've got something that has to be done in the next week or two. I mean it'll be part of your working day, just something different from normal.'

'That's fine. What is it?'

'Meeting a possible client for a potential private art purchase. Basically you discover her interests, leave her a card with a phone number. And that's it.'

'I see. I think I could manage that. I'd hate to mess it up.'

'I'm pretty busy right now. I've another Africa trip to sort out. But mainly it's because I've met this client before and we just don't get on. I'm not sure why. Somehow the personal chemistry doesn't work. She's a doctor actually. I seem to threaten her somehow. I'm sure you two will get on fine. Anyway we've got a hint that she is very keen on getting hold of a Kandinsky, so we just need to sound her out. So what do you think? Are you up for it?'

'A Kandinsky? Is she that wealthy?'

'I know -- there must be pots of inherited money, but she might just be after a good print. Our role is to help her sort out her interests then act as a sounding board for the market, find out what she wants, find out what funds are available, feel out possibilities. Our firm does all that sort of thing, you would simply do the initial discussion. I'll make sure you're well briefed.'

It sounded quite a challenge but of course I said, 'OK. That's fine.'

'Great -- oh, and I must remember to fit in a visit to your Grandfather....I'm looking forward to that.'

When I got home, I looked up Africa-Read-Write on the web. A drab site with loads of text with far too much detail, a few small photos and an address to send cheque donations. There was no sense of the potential audience. I couldn't see Jill's hand in it at all.

5

A few days later, I was making a coffee for myself in the office when a small miracle happened. I spotted two visitors through the office window. I slipped into the gallery and stood at the receptionist's desk. I willed them to need some help, for when Jill was out, I was getting sick of being alone, with a none-job.

It was a middle-aged couple, both comfortably built, but neither of them my idea of art gallery types -- a bit loud. The woman looked as if she was entering an alien world. I rapped my knuckles for stereotyping them and tried to look approachable but not pushy. The man, a going-to-fat forty-year-old, was in a loud purple shirt and too-tight black jeans. He looked a bit sleazy. He had a flat, used face but rather impressive wavy greying hair, standing out from his head beneath a dark purple cap.

He started 'explaining' the red abstracts to his companion with expansive gestures, almost as if he was the painter. The woman had a slightly puffed but jolly face -- and was heavily made up. Her colourful dress had swirls of what could be giant leaves with branches coiling round her. She looked bemused by the large red abstracts -- and the explanation.

As they got nearer to the desk, I could hear more. I thought he might be putting on a show for me.

'This one, one of my favourites by the way -- this artist is really inspired. It's all blood, rivers of blood, -- death and birth -- wombs and menstruation.'

The woman nodded to him but glanced helplessly in my direction, so I stepped forward.

'They are quite challenging, aren't they....'

The woman curled her lip and made a gesture of helplessness with her hands. 'I just can't make any sense of them. I can't see anything in them.'

She had rather a high voice but quite confident. 'And why are they all red?'

The man stepped in. 'Actually, they're not unlike my own paintings...'

'Well at least yours have more colour in them – different colours that is.'

She paused and looked at me for support.

'The artist says on his web site that they're about states of mind. This one is called Despair Three.'

She laughed. 'Despair -- that's what I feel with these. But why three?'

I laughed back and nodded, for I found these paintings oppressive. Jill had 'discovered' the artist -- and given him a six month exhibition.

The man stepped towards me. 'Eva isn't really into art but I just had to show her our gallery.'

'Right, that's good. Sorry -- did you say *our* gallery?'

He smirked. 'Our family owns it. Julius, my father. Then there's sister Jill. And obviously I get involved now and then.'

'Oh I see. I'm new here. I've only really met Jill so far -- and your father, briefly. So you're Jill's brother....'

Eva smiled -- new girl to new girl.

The man offered me his hand. 'Half-brother actually. Same dad, different mums. I'm Baz -- and I'm not the black sheep of the family like some might have you believe. And this is Eva.'

I shook hands with both of them. Eva had a cheery smile and an attractive warmth about her. I was unsure about Baz. His flowing locks, purple cap and shirt made an effect -- and he seemed lively. So this was the son of Julius Carruthers...

'Did you say you paint?'

'Yes. Abstracts. About the subconscious mind. Similar subject matter to these really, but very different.'

Eve echoed him, 'Yes, very different.'

'Sounds interesting....'

'Tell that to my sister. I've been trying to get some of them into this gallery for an age. They'd fit the space. They really would.'

After an awkward pause, I had to say, 'I'm only a temp so I've got no say on hanging policy.'

Eva said, 'They're very good, Baz's paintings, full of different colours. They're rather like one of those oil films you see after rain. Know what I mean?'

'Eva's on the right lines; the spectrum is one of my inspirations. I'll bring one or two in to show you if you like...'

'You need to talk with Jill about that.....'

'She doesn't want to know. She hasn't even been to look at them -- but if I get the chance, I'll bring one in to show you...er..'

'Sadie.'

'Nice name.' He was out to charm me. 'There isn't any chance of a coffee round here is there?'

My instinct was to say no, but then he was Jill's brother. 'Well -- possibly but I'm not sure we've got any milk left.'

That was a lie, but I felt cornered.

'Why don't you two have a look at the portraits while I see what I can do?'

Eva looked along the line of geometric heads and said, 'Portraits? Is that what they are?'

I went to set up Jill's coffee machine and got out

the milk from the small fridge. After a few minutes of further arm waving by Baz, I rescued Eva and led them into the office. Baz had a nosy round while Eva took one of the seats then asked if she could help.

Baz tried to open a filing cabinet drawer. My heart sank. I thought of Sean, whose visit I hadn't mentioned to Jill. She had never mentioned either Baz or Sean to me. I suddenly thought -- these two in Jill's office could be anyone. Am I too trusting?

'Locked - that's sensible I suppose. I was just going to check on the filing..... never Jill's top skill. I guess you do that now?'

I tried to take control. 'I'm afraid there's no biscuits or anything.' A lie as Jill's chocolate biscuits were hidden away. 'Where are you going to sit, Baz?'

'Anywhere you like, dear.'

After a pause, Eva said, 'Cosy little office, isn't it...' At this point I was really uncomfortable. Baz and I ignored her comment, which was rubbish anyway.

As the coffee machine worked, he said, 'So you're new here. Like it? You're not exactly rushed off your feet, are you.'

'I'm not complaining - it's a job.'

Eva said, 'Good for you!'

'I suppose you need qualifications to get a job like this...'

He was beginning to get on my nerves.

'I've got an Art History degree if that's what you mean...'

'Now that's impressive. I'll definitely bring one of my paintings in.'

'I will really need to check that out with Jill first...'

At last the machine gurgled and I was able to pour out the coffees.

Eva seemed a nice woman so I tried to rescue the situation.

'So those paintings aren't really your type of art?'

Eva squirmed a little, closed her eyes and shook her head, 'Oh no.'

'Eva's an opera freak, aren't you darling. She dragged me off to something the other night and I hardly heard a thing for her sobs.'

They both laughed. Eva said to me, 'La Boheme. It gets me every time. I don't know why I go. It's torture, but it's wonderful.'

There was some scuttling in the gallery. Surely not further visitors? Then young Harry, Jill's son, appeared at the office door. He stared in at us, then ran off.

Baz groaned. 'That's Jill's lad - there's gonna be trouble...'

Then Jill appeared at the office door, holding the little boy's hand. She looked in and almost glared.

'Baz, what a surprise. Well -- sorry to interrupt the three of you, I'm sure...'

I felt guilty -- but why should I? Baz had given me little choice but to make coffee.

'I thought that -- well -- it's not every day that a member of the family firm visits.'

Jill said rather sharply, 'Baz isn't involved in the business, are you dear?' She turned to Eva, 'I don't think we've met.'

Eva stood and said, 'I'm Eva. I'm -- a friend of Baz.' They shook hands then Eva put out her hand to the boy who was hovering behind Jill.

'And who are you? What a smart young man......'

Baz suddenly swept the little boy up and lifted him high. He announced over the boy's squeals, 'This is

Harry - the black bombshell.'

Jill said bluntly. 'Put him down Baz - and don't call him that. Let him shake Eva's hand.'

Baz lowered him and still holding him, turned so that Eva could shake his hand.

Eva beamed. 'Hello Harry - how are you? And what have you been up to today?'

'Shopping, playing on my tablet. Getting up, that was the first thing - er, what else Mum?'

Jill rolled her eyes. 'That's fine darling. Eva doesn't want all the details...'

After an awkward pause, Eva said to Jill, 'I've got two of my own - and two grandchildren Harry's sort of age, a boy and a girl.'

'Really. Well look, it's nice to have met you, Eva, but Sadie and I have work to do...'

'Yes....I'm sure you have,' said Baz, knowingly. 'We'd better be off...' To Harry, still in his arms he said, 'But we could always stay to play with you while these two work?'

Jill stepped forward to reclaim her son, 'No. He'd get far too excited -- and then there'd be tears. Harry's going to do some quiet drawing for us.... Sadie, will you see Eva and Baz out please.'

Baz rolled his eyes and I did as I was told.

On the walk down the gallery, he asked, 'Hitting it off with Cruella de Vil?'

I was thrown by this but Eva came to my rescue, 'Don't be silly Baz. I'm sure they get on fine.' To me she said, 'That's sibling rivalry for you...'

Baz harrumphed. 'You don't know the half of it!'

Back in the office, Harry was busy starting a drawing. As I entered, Jill drew me out of Harry's hearing.

'Look Sadie, you were hardly to know, but my brother's a scrounger. Just don't let him in this office again - alright?'

'Yes - fine. But how do I stop him?'

'Simple. You're out of coffee and are doing some urgent research work for me.'

'Right. I can manage that.'

'Good. He was always pestering Julius to let him into the business but he messes things up, so now we keep him out.'

'So there's little contact?'

'Tariq and I keep well away from him. You saw how he was with Harry; he's impossible.'

'I see. Baz said you had the same dad and different mothers.'

'He did, did he? Yes well Julius deserted the first, that's Baz's mother, then divorced the second, my mother. Baz has always been a pain in the backside. Julius has tried to fix him up in jobs, but now he won't have him anywhere near the business. He's not reliable and he drinks -- so be warned'.

'Right. I'm warned.'

6

    I knew that my Grandfather would be pleased to have Jill visit him. Walter would do anything for me. He'd helped me through university and now we only lived twenty minutes walk from each other, he in his handsome terrace, me with Mel in the small flat she said I would eventually inherit. Walter lived alone, except for Freud, the cat – and Alice, the part-time cook and housekeeper. I visited him most weeks, especially when Mel had her boyfriend over. Mel sometimes asked me what I would do with my inheritance when Walter died but I couldn't think in those terms.

    I was close to Walter and I wanted him to live for ages. I felt his loneliness. We got on well, talking about art, often looking at TV programmes about art. He loved Klee and Macke -- and of the Brits, David Hockney and Francis Bacon. Being almost house-bound with a heart condition, he no longer got out to galleries.

    He retained his looks -- a long face with heavy lidded eyes, white goatee beard and moustache, still streaked with black -- and rather full lips. He must have been a good kisser in his day.

    I was deep in my favourite leather chair in his large lounge. I had spent so many hours in this room, my safe haven, especially since my Grandmother had died. The afternoon sun flooded on to Walter with Freud on his lap and the light cut across the splendid cubist painting over the fireplace, a striking angular head. I sometimes wondered if one day I would own it, but not soon, I hoped.

'Well, bring Jill round. I don't mind chatting to her. Do I have to buy a painting from her to get you a permanent job? Is that the idea?'

'No Grandfather -- definitely not. I would hate that. The job's temporary and when the regular person has her baby, I'll be out. There's not really work enough for one - there are hardly any visitors.'

'Why do they keep the place open?'

'Good question. Please don't ask Jill that.'

'The web site's awful and the art on it is – mixed. I don't mind the portraits but some of those abstracts are banal.'

'I know.'

'And you have to try to sell them? Anyway, bring her round. If you like her, she must be alright.'

I should never never have introduced Jill to Walter. Quite possibly I wouldn't be marooned on another continent now if I'd had any idea of what would happen. I was too inexperienced to realise that as a temporary employee, Jill would use me to get her hands on a potential client. And as for Walter, start talking to him about Francis Bacon -- and he loses all balance. So naturally they got on very well. In fact once they got together, I felt irrelevant.

Jill had taken much greater care over clothes and make-up than for my job interview. Her black dress and scarlet jacket were almost dramatic.

On the way in she murmured to me, 'I've just come from a presentation -- hope this isn't over the top...'

Her charm was all focused on Walter. I had told him about Jill's Africa charity and this triggered his interest. She described ARW, Africa-Read-Write, in colourful terms. Her passionate concern for the girls was shining through. Eventually they got on to paintings and Walter was fairly blunt about the web site.

'You're right, Walter. It needs more work. At the moment the web site and gallery are just ticking over. That's why Sadie's not exactly overworked. Our main focus is on outside clients, using our knowledge of the art world for their benefit. The web site is misleading because we actually deal with a much wider range of art.'

I wanted to say -- let me redesign the web site.

Jill continued with her pitch. 'If a painting is on the market, we can bid for it - and through our contacts, we sometimes have advance notice of a painting approaching the market, even plant a seed in the mind of the current owner. In a way the world's our oyster.'

'Which is why you're here...'

'Yes but I'm not here to do a hard sell or anything. Sadie's mentioned that you are a collector and I was fascinated to meet someone who actually knew Francis Bacon.'

'Oh, she told you.'

They both smiled in my direction. They were delighted, but I, who loathed Bacon's paintings, was not.

'Not exactly knew -- I used to drink in the same bar, that's all. He was a tricky sort of fellow, a waspish tongue. He held court. I kept out of his way, but listened in. And now, I suppose I've got a bit, not exactly obsessed, but he's still very important to me.'

I had heard all this before. For myself I was disturbed by Bacon's mixture of sadism, despair and sexual abuse. How could anyone like these paintings? Obsessed - surely not? I always drew back but Jill seemed completely at ease.

'There must be thousands of people like me who dream of owning a Bacon. I know it's foolish, but I've wanted one as long as I remember….I know I'm mad!'

'You seem to me very sane Walter. But you also need to be extremely wealthy and possibly looking for a long term investment.'

'I'm not that rich, but I'd love one of his self-portraits. They don't often come on the market, do they?'

'They don't, but if you want I'll explore my contacts. Put it out on the radar, anonymously of course.'

Walter sat back. He caught my eye and I could tell from his look he was thinking – I know I'm being foolish. Then he turned back to Jill

'Let's be honest with each other Jill. I don't want to waste your time...'

'It's fine. There may be options apart from purchasing at absurd prices. For example rental is not unknown. Also in the Bacon market I know there are some marvellous copies...'

'Forgeries, you mean?'

'I mean painted copies and also excellent digital prints. I've seen some convincing work.'

Walter was nodding at Jill, 'I never thought about anything but an original, but I'll seriously consider any ideas you have.' I began to realise that a strong rapport was emerging.

Still nodding, he said, 'Jill, we ought to offer you some coffee.'

'I'd love some. In the gallery Sadie keeps me well supplied….'

Walter turned to me, 'Well then -- are you happy to fix some for us, darling?'

So I was dismissed from the grown-up room and dispatched to the kitchen, telling myself not to be silly. Of course they wanted coffee. Alice wasn't around, so obviously it fell to me. I should have suggested it. As I got the things together, I glanced back through the open door. They were in close conversation and then the kettle drowned out all noise. When it switched off I could overhear occasional phrases -- that end of the market -- your mobile number.

As I carried in the tray, the two sat back in their chairs.

'And does Sadie always have to make the coffee in the gallery? That seems hard.'

'Well I supply the coffee and the chocolate biscuits, so I think all's fair.'

And the conversation stayed on my work in the galleries, in a slightly jokey and patronising way, as if the Bacon self-portrait needed no further discussion -- or at least none involving me. That was the impression I had and of course later events confirmed it.

With business complete and coffee gulped down, Jill had to rush off to collect Harry. On leaving, all she said to Walter was, 'If we discover anything of interest, we'll be in contact...'

After I took Jill to the door, I sat down again with Walter.

'So what did you think of her?

'She's charming, absolutely charming. It must be good working for her.'

'Yes, she is super to be with. And I know her

husband or partner -- I'm not sure which -- and her son.'

'Really? I don't care much for this husband-partner business.'

Walter seemed a little distant, perhaps running over the conversation with Jill.

'So what did you both decide about the Bacon self-portrait?'

He looked at me as if I was challenging him. 'Oh that. Nothing's going to come of that. Who wants a copy for heaven's sake? No, Jill's a very attractive person and it was interesting to meet your boss. But I expect that will be the end of it.'

'Right. So it was a bit of a waste of time?'

'Not at all my dear. It's been an interesting afternoon, but for me slightly exhausting. To be honest, I need to lie down and have a snooze.'

He certainly looked weary.

'I don't want to drive you away but I need to take my pills then retreat for an hour or two.'

So I let myself out, not really knowing what had been agreed between them, if anything. I had long known that Walter was defensive about his interest in Bacon and that he can be quite evasive at times. I told myself that being excluded from the grownups talk happened; don't build it up into something big. I got that completely wrong.

7

It was great that Jill wanted me to take on some of her client visits. It was sad that this was triggered by Tariq's illness, but a variation on the gallery job was so welcome.

I parked in the leafy road so that I could walk up the drive to the large house, whose owner wanted a Kandinsky. Jill had given me some idea of this clever Doctor Sophie Wilson with whom her chemistry didn't work -- and that worried me. I had rehearsed the task carefully; Jill and I had done mock discussions, but an intelligent woman who disliked Jill was a daunting prospect. I felt that a man might be more easily handled.

The handsome Victorian house was draped in ivy and looked well maintained, as was the simple flower garden around a beautifully kept lawn.

The door was opened by a smart woman, self-possessed, erect posture, a little taller than me. She wore a business type suit. Her hair was blond-pageboy style, rather dashing for someone perhaps in her late forties. Her square pale face and blue eyes were dominated by elegant spectacles.

I put on my best chirpy front, 'Good morning. I'm Sadie from Gallery Elite.'

She smiled in a 'next patient' sort of way, 'Ah good. Come in.' Nothing given away.

She led me into a traditionally decorated lounge and indicated that we should sit down on easy chairs in the large bay window overlooking the lawn.

She lent towards me and adopted a rather confidential manner, 'I hope you don't mind my

41

saying, but you're younger than you sound on the phone -- unless the genes have been exceptionally kind to you ...'

'I expect you spoke to Jill, my boss.'

'Jill Carruthers? Ah, I see.' It wasn't clear to me what she saw. 'She's the manager and you're the salesperson. Is that it?'

'Actually, I'm an Art Consultant. I know a certain amount about the visual arts and I hope this meeting can be more of a discussion. If a purchase happens eventually, that's all to the good.'

'Bravo -- I approve of that! So tell me about Gallery Elite. I've seen the website of course...' Her tone said it all. I needed to take control of it somehow.

'I know -- we're working on that. The art acquisition side of the business is separate from the gallery.'

'That's a relief.'

So back to my script, 'Well -- we have a lot of experience in the art market. We know how to locate works of art, mainly paintings -- and to talk with potential vendors. We try to bring people together who don't quite realise they need each other.'

'Interesting.... I'm not at all sure you'll be able to help me but I'll tell you exactly what I want. My father has a passion for Kandinsky. I know how much they cost on the open market and I haven't got that sort of money. So what do I do?'

'There may be possibilities. Is he into any particular aspect of Kandinsky, like a particular period?'

'Oh yes, he's fascinated by a particular painting. Composition 12. That's its name.'

'I know Kandinsky's paintings quite well. He's a genius. I must have seen photos of Composition 12.

Do you know who owns it?'

'I think it's in private ownership somewhere near Dorking. The name of the family is Simpson. They bought it six years ago.'

'And you want to know if they could be persuaded to sell it.'

'Basically yes – and for less than its market value.'

'Do you happen to know what that is?'

'More than ten million -- much more than I have access to.'

'I see.'

'So…I'm wasting your time, aren't I?'

'We need to explore possibilities. Do you mind my asking how much you have access to?'

'Let's say an order of magnitude down from its value. You probably think I'm deluded -- but for my father, well, things are becoming difficult, let's say a little urgent. He's quite old and very determined. I'll be frank with you. I either want that painting -- or an excellent copy.'

'I see. Is it important which?'

'He may be a bit deranged, but he's not stupid. He'd see through a photographic-type print. I know there's lots of those available cheaply on the web. Visually he's still sharp -- so the other options are what I want to explore…'

'Well first I wouldn't dismiss the photographic reproductions. The best are fantastic – especially when printed on canvas and well framed.'

'Right, and other options?'

'A painted copy would cost a lot more but might be more convincing.'

She raised an eyebrow. 'Are we talking forgery here?'

I couldn't tell whether she was encouraging or

provoking me, but I tried to sound neutral, 'I wouldn't use that word. You're trying to please your father, not deceive the art market.'

'True.'

'If my memory serves me right, Kandinsky died during the Second World War -- so we might be just on the wrong side of the 70 year copyright rule for a copy, but there are ways around that....Do you want me to explore possibilities?'

'Please. And can I get to see examples of the two – the photo and the painted copy – and what about the relative prices?'

'I can get examples to you but I want to mention another possibility. We could approach the owners for a loan of the original, for three or four years say....'

'I'd never have thought of that. Why should they agree?'

'If the price was right – and they had something good to fill the gap...'

'I see. Well, thinking of my father, a few years might be about right. I know I sound brutal but the end of life is such a lottery.'

'I know. My Grandfather is -- well, has a heart condition.'

'So you know what I mean.'

We talked about this more and established a sort of bond, then I summarised what we would do next.

'Someone should ring you. In a few days.'

'Of course. Who is this someone?'

'At this stage, I'm not sure. It might be me -- or one of my colleagues from Gallery Elite.'

'I'd rather it was you. And when you ring, if you get my father, just leave a name and number for me to call back. This is to be a complete surprise for him.'

I walked away from the house feeling so happy – I'd done it. I felt comfortable about my performance and I knew I could do it again. The doctor had at least a million so she was going to get something impressive for her father, even if it was not the real thing. I could hardly wait to tell Jill.

In the debriefing session, she quizzed me closely about the nuances of my discussion.

'You did well, very well, especially given the spikiness of that particular lady'.

'Thanks'. I was still very susceptible to praise from Jill. 'So what happens now?'

'I'll take her over from here.'

'But I thought you and she weren't…didn't see eye to eye.'

'That's true but this one could get complicated.'

'But she said she wanted me to get back to her…'

'Did she? Look Sadie, this is where it could get really complex. Julius or I will handle this but don't worry. I'll let you know what happens…'

So if I was edging towards making myself indispensible, I was not always going to get my own way.

I mentioned the comment about the Gallery Elite web site. 'Dr Wilson was quite critical of it. It needs to be a tool for attracting clients and giving them confidence, don't you agree Jill?'

'You're right. Sean does it at present. I wonder if you ought to have an input there?'

Jill didn't know that I'd met Sean and had already made a tentative link over the web site.

'It needs a stronger sense of audience, doesn't it….'

'You're right. I'll mention that to Sean and we'll sort something out.'

8

Next morning, just after opening, I was at the reception desk catching up on Facebook, when Jill's half-brother Baz appeared at the gallery door. No cap this time, just his surprisingly long locks over his rather podgy body. He was almost on tiptoe and mouthed to me, '*Is she in?*' pointing at the office window. I shook my head and he left, then re-entered holding a wrapped-up painting.

He marched down the gallery clutching the painting. 'Sadie, I really want you to see one of my pieces. I want your honest opinion.'

My heart sank. I walked down the gallery towards him.

'Baz, you do know that I don't decide what goes on these walls.'

'I know. It's the family gallery and I'm not expecting any special treatment. I just want your honest opinion.'

'I'm only a temp. As people keep reminding me.'

'You're an art graduate. That's what's important to me.'

I hesitated. I didn't want to hurt the man but I certainly was not going to annoy Jill, who called him a scrounger.

'What if Jill comes in and finds you and your painting?'

'I'll vanish before she comes... When is she coming in anyway? '

'As it happens, I don't think she'll be in till tomorrow morning. But she could change her mind.'

'So fate's on our side. I don't want to put you on

46

the spot Sadie, so I'm going to leave it with you so
you can have a good look. I'll come back later then
just tell me what you think.'

I felt cornered. I was curious to see the painting,
which I feared would be ghastly, so I was relieved to
not have to give an immediate reaction.

'Alright. Pass it over. I'll look at it when I have
some spare time later. Remember we close at five.'

He gave me a big goofy smile and seemed about
to hug me, but I placed his painting between us.

I said firmly, 'See you later...'

'Great. You will. By the way it's called
Subconscious 2. And Sadie – in advance, thank you.'
He looked so grateful. I walked away from him just to
make sure he knew he was dismissed.

The painting was about a metre square, unframed
and wrapped in a cloth. I took it into the office,
unwrapped it and placed it on the table. It was a bold
acrylic, with large sweeps of primary colour edging
into darker areas. Dramatic, quite like a Hubble image
of a huge cosmic event. At first I couldn't tell which
way round to look at it. To my surprise, I rather liked
it. For me it was much better than the red abstracts
hanging in the gallery -- but I didn't plan to say that to
Baz. On impulse, I took a snap of the painting on my
phone, then wrapped it up and tucked it behind the
filing cabinet.

Around three in the afternoon, a man almost fell
through the door into the gallery. It was Baz and he
was drunk.

He stumbled along the gallery towards me, then
mumbled, 'Who are you? - oh - forgot your name....'

'Sadie?'

'Sade, yes I remember - I'm not myself today. Where's Jill...'

I tried not to panic. He glared at me, 'Well -- is her majesty in today?'

'Baz – I told you earlier, Jill's not around...'

'Not available - I see - no I don't see actually - do you mean she's in that bloody office but won't see her own brother?'

I wavered, then said, 'She's not in the building.'

'She's not gone off to fucking Africa again - don't tell me that - please.'

'...er -- I'm not sure where she is, but she's definitely not in fucking Africa.'

My sarcasm was lost on him.

'Well tell her that her brother called and I'll come back tomorrow...and I'll expect her to be here.'

'Right. I'll pass on the message...'

He had totally forgotten his painting.

He started up again, 'She's off to bloody Africa again, isn't she - I knew it -- what a bloody waste - she's wasting the fucking family money -- she won't make any difference - the whole bloody continent's messed up...'

'Look Baz, try to be sensible. She's concentrating on a few villages, on girls' education.'

'Really! How nice! And what about the other million villages? They don't matter I suppose – it's a farce - and what about the boys? They don't matter either - she turns the world upside down and throws away money on a handful of black girls. It drives me fucking mad.'

I glared at him and almost shouted, 'You're completely wrong. At least her heart is in the right place...'

'Oh is it? How nice! Saint bloody Jill, that's what I call her.'

This time I kept silent. I was shocked by his name for her.

He stumbled around looking at the same paintings he'd been extolling to Eva. 'What's this supposed to be? It doesn't make sense. Daft, it's fucking daft. All these blotches? It looks like somebody's bleeding. Good God -- do people pay for these? This place is a farce. Somebody ought to sort this lot out.'

He was stumbling around in front of the red canvases he'd been extolling to Eva. I desperately wanted to stop him parading round the gallery, with me in attendance.

But at the next painting, he stopped then mumbled, 'Got anything to drink?.....don't bother, there's something here.'

He drew out of his shoulder bag the remains of a bottle of whisky and emptied it down his throat. He was unsteady on his feet and in turning, tripped over and fell heavily to the ground. He was not a lightweight but seemed unhurt. I stood back to see what he would do. He said 'Oh God', lay back awkwardly and closed his eyes. He continued breathing, noisily.

So what now? It was mid-afternoon. I struggled with my basic first aid. With difficulty, I rolled him on his side. He was breathing noisily and had a pulse. He seemed to be either sleeping or unconscious or just dead drunk. He stank of alcohol and sweat.

I couldn't just leave him there. If someone came, I could always say he was an installation -- silly joke! I could ring Mel; her boyfriend or her brother Kyle might be there, though Mel and I could probably manage to get him into a taxi. I retreated to the reception desk and the phone. This was Jill's problem, obviously, so I decided to ring her. No response on the mobile but the landline was answered by Tariq.

'Tariq -- is that you? I need some help. Jill's brother's here -- he's drunk. He's passed out on the floor.'

'Baz? Oh bloody hell. I'll come round -- I'll be a few minutes. I'll just leave Harry with a neighbour. Can you cope alright till I come?'

'He's asleep -- on the floor. Or unconscious....'

'Does he need an ambulance?'

' I don't think so – he's breathing. I'll keep an eye on him...'

'OK -- I won't be long.'

After phoning I stayed at the reception desk for a while staring at the prone figure half way along the gallery. I could hear his breathing even from this distance. After a minute, I thought I'd look more closely -- I approached him quietly. He was slumped on one side, shoulders forward, both hands resting on the lower knee. He was breathing loudly. His long hair was over his eyes. He looked extremely uncomfortable but I was definitely not going to disturb him.

I slowly walked all the way round him. I stared at his hands and the lower part of his face -- and his shapeless body imagined beneath his clothes. I felt like a voyeur – and had a queasy disgust at him and myself. To feel power over this silly man was strange. I hate violence -- but could easily have kicked him hard in the backside. Then the better part of me said – grow up -- this is Jill's brother. I returned to my desk.

At last Tariq rushed in. He stopped at the body,

felt the forehead and then looked at me, 'He's OK. Are you alright?'

It was a vast relief to have him here. 'I'm fine -- he didn't try anything. He was going on endlessly about Jill and Africa.'

He picked up the bottle. 'He stinks. I knew he drank but I've never seen him like this before. Well, he can't stay here. We'd better get him into the pickup.'

'Do you know where he lives?'

'It's not far.'

Tariq started looking in Baz's shoulder bag.

'Here's his wallet -- not much there. Hang on to his bag while I get him up. Right my man, here we go -- up you get. Let's get you to the door.'

Baz allowed himself to be helped up, leaning against Tariq. He half opened his eyes then bellowed out, 'Who the hell are you? Get your filthy hands off me you fucking thief.'

He tried to take a swing at Tariq but could hardly stay upright.

He made another lunge. 'Get the hell out of it -- back to where you came from.'

He tried to glare at Tariq but just looked pathetic.

I was shocked. 'That's vile. Can't we just push him out of the door and leave him on the pavement.'

Tariq snorted. 'I don't think so. It's the family – Jill's the success, he's the failure. We need to get him home.'

Baz had given up the fight and seemed conscious again. He grabbed his bag out of my hands. Tariq manhandled him through the door and on to the pavement.

'We'll get him into the pickup, then belt him into the passenger seat.'

A few passers-by stared at us. One young guy

seemed to think this was a kidnap.

I called out, 'Sorry -- it's alright. Our friend's a bit unwell...'

We got him on to the front bench of Tariq's pickup. Something in me wanted to see this little drama through to the end.

'I could come with you, help sort him out. What do you think?'

'What about the gallery?'

'It's alright. I'll just lock up...'

It was far from closing time but the chances of anyone arriving were slight.

'I can manage him by myself, really...I've done worse...'

He was right. I had to be sensible. Tariq looked at me more closely.

'Look, you come if you want to -- I wouldn't mind the company. How quickly can you lock up?'

'Three minutes?'

'OK -- you're on.'

I rushed in and did the fastest lock up ever, picked up Baz's painting and rushed out to find him asleep again, strapped in. Tariq got out so that I could slide in between the two men, but first I pushed the painting behind the seats..

Once I got my breath back, I realised I was crushed between the two men.

Tariq said, 'You OK?'

'Yes fine. Is Baz OK?'

'Dozed off - what a wreck. What's that? A painting?'

I whispered, 'It's Baz's. He brought it in earlier for me to -- give my opinion. He didn't want Jill to know.'

'Right. I didn't see anything. Is it any good?'

'Better than you'd expect from someone in this state. He left it this morning and was coming to see what I thought, but he obviously got a bit distracted.'

'He was worried about what you'd say...'

'No. Really?'

'He's sensitive despite the bluster. I think he's a bit paranoid actually...and given his background....'

We set off. On the left hand bends, I had to endure stinking Baz sliding close and occasionally I had to push his head off my shoulder.

Quietly, I whispered to Tariq, 'I can hardly believe he's Jill's brother....'

'Different mothers. Julius was young when he had Baz, like in his teens - and he abandoned the mother. They only met when Baz was in his twenties. Julius had been....otherwise occupied...'

'Do you mean he was in prison?'

'Oh, you knew?'

'No, it was the way you said it...'

'Am I that obvious? Alright then, you don't know what I said about Julius and I don't know about Baz's painting. A deal?'

'A deal. So what's happening now between Baz and his dad?'

'They don't see much of each other. Baz is still trying to work his way into the business, as far as I know.'

'Jill told me he's a scrounger. He came round with his girlfriend a few days ago and half pretended to own the place.'

'That's him. He wants to be in on the business and Julius won't have it. Here's the block where he lives -- let's see where I can park...this'll do.'

Once we had eased him out of the car, Baz came

to life enough to stand and stumble along.

Tariq said, 'Baz - have you got your key?'

'Course I've got my bloody keys...'

Eventually he fished out a bunch of keys and handed them to Tariq. He was recovering now, enough to walk himself into the lift.

On the way up Tariq said, 'Feeling better now?'

'I'm fine. What the hell are you two doing here?'

Tariq winked at me. 'Didn't you invite us up for a coffee?'

'Did I? I don't remember that.' We reached the top floor and made our way to Baz's flat door. 'I didn't know you had a new girlfriend - where's Jill anyway? Does she know what you're up to?'

'Baz, don't be rude.' Tariq's accent was so proper, but with a northern twang. 'This is Sadie who runs the gallery where you collapsed on the floor, drunk....'

'Did I? Oh God...don't let Jill know, will you.'

'You brought this painting to show me, remember?'

He seemed to see the cloth wrapper for the first time, 'Did I? Oh God, I remember now. So what did you think?'

'Not bad at all. Bold. You ought to do more...'

He turned to me and gave me a big smile. He was thrilled but turned it into a shrug, 'I have – I'll show you them.'

As Tariq struggled with finding the flat door key, I heard loud music. Eventually the door swung open and we were hit by a blast of modern jazz. Through the hall, in the living room, there was a man in shorts on the floor. He was doing press-ups and looked extremely fit. Up - down - up - down, quickly, muscles standing out on his arms. If he was aware of the open door, he ignored it. The three of us gaped at the body – up, down..

Then Tariq got hold of Baz by the shoulders and hissed at him, 'What the hell is Sean doing here?'

'Get off me! If you must know, we're doing some work together.'

Sean and scrounger Baz? This was the Sean who had visited the gallery a few days ago and had designed the flashy gallery web site. Sean and Tariq were colleagues -- of course, so why the anger?

After a few moments, Sean looked in our direction, leapt up, lowered the sound then walked gracefully towards us. I tried not to look at his body but splendid was the only word - and didn't he know it. His head was more striking than good-looking - cropped head, a wide sensual sort of mouth, a goatee - and dark eyes with a tinge of violet.

'Hi - I didn't know you were having visitors Baz. I'd have showered earlier. Hi Sadie -- I haven't forgotten about the web site....Tariq - how's life?' With a glance in my direction, he said, 'I see you're not wasting time...'

I felt indignant, but couldn't find the right words.

Tariq blurted out, 'And I didn't know you two were that friendly.' He seemed to have become very tense.

Sean was unconcerned. 'I come round for a chat now and then....'

Tariq muttered, 'That must be cosy...'

Baz glared at Tariq, 'What do you mean - cosy? You've got a bloody cheek.'

Sean rolled his eyes. 'Let it go Baz. I don't think lover-boy meant anything.'

I thought that Tariq blushed. I felt thrown by being seen as 'Tariq's', and I didn't really understand what was going on. Anyway Sean ignored me and talked directly to Tariq.

'We get on fine actually, Baz and I, when he keeps off the booze...'

'Oh come off it Sean - I don't drink every night...'

'Baz and I have some little plots to hatch together.' Baz nodded and smirked at Tariq.

Tariq said, 'What does that mean?

'All in good time Tariq, all in good time.'

Tariq hesitated, then in a burst almost shouted, 'So why the hell do you come round here to do your exercises?'

Sean placed a hand on Baz's shoulder. 'Just filling in time -- till his lordship comes home...'

Then Sean steered Baz into the flat and moved to close the door.

Baz blurted out, 'Hang on. Sadie wants to see my other paintings...'

Sean continued to draw Baz in. 'Some other time -- they're on their way...'

As he began to close the door, he said to Tariq and me, 'By the way, you two look good together. See you soon.'

He winked and shut the door in our faces.

Tariq, very tense, just stared at the closed door. I had no idea what he was thinking but guessed I was not part of it.

After what seemed an age, I said, 'What does that mean? He can't think that...'

He came to and turned to the stairs. 'Ignore him. He's a bastard....'

'I don't trust him. He seems to be playing games.'

'That's one way of putting it. I'd keep away from him if I were you. You probably don't want my advice...'

'Tariq, I think I do.' I told myself to calm down, 'Anyway you work together with him, don't you? What sort of work do you do?'

'Oh, Julius-type projects, fetching and carrying. Now, shall I give you a lift somewhere?'

'The next tube station is fine…'

On the way, he deflected further questions about Sean and we settled for chatter about Harry.

That evening, I got a text from Jill saying my predecessor was not coming back and offering me a six month contract.

9

Two weeks later, I was at work, feeling bored, when Jill arrived at the gallery with Marion, the ARW administrator who I had met when babysitting Harry. Marion marched slightly behind Jill and glanced briefly at the paintings but without interest. She looked ready to take command more of a hockey pitch than an art gallery. Her large square spectacles above a wide pursed mouth made her look rather grim.

Jill was flustered. 'Sadie - we're having a meeting in the office. Don't let anyone disturb us.'

I nodded but thought, be serious Jill, nobody comes to the gallery anyway.

I said, 'Hi Marion, nice to see you again.' Not true, but I wanted to get involved in the charity and if that meant making an effort, I'd do it. I got a curt nod in return.

The meeting went on for about forty minutes. I couldn't hear their actual words but the tension was obvious. Marion spoke in a deep penetrating voice impossible to ignore. She sounded so pedantic.

Eventually the office door opened and she was still talking.

'….of course I'm very disappointed. You've let ARW down. The town is expecting a new school and now I have to tell them it's not going to happen.'

'I know Marion -- but I'll be there with you - I'll take the blame…'

They walked past me as if I wasn't there.

'I should hope so! And what about those girls - and their futures - or lack of it. It's unthinkable what they have to endure.'

'I feel dreadful about it. I should never have made that promise. This is the first time it's happened and it'll be the last. I'm certain of that.'

'I hope so, Jill. It's a hard lesson for all of us. I believed the funds were secure and I was completely wrong. Now we've got to face the consequences....'

'Yes, I'm sorry -- I really am.....we're on the same flight, aren't we?'

'Of course. I'll send you an email about where to meet me.'

And she abruptly walked away, down the length of the gallery and left without looking back.

Jill stared after her. Then she remembered that I was there. She wiped her brow in affected relief - and came back to my desk in dejection.

'You couldn't do me a coffee could you? Make it two - I need consoling.'

As we went into the office, she said, 'I knew that was going to be difficult but...oh dear me.'

As I made the coffee, Jill talked.

'The trouble is that I promised more than I can deliver -- I mean in funds. We were hoping to start on a new school, but we're going to be short.'

'Did you say the funds were from your inheritance?'

'Did I? -- yes, of course. But it's locked up in trusts and bonds and things - and with the recession and everything - it's all got very complicated. And Marion finds it impossible to adjust. It should only be a short delay. I hope.' Jill slumped into silence.

'She seems a bit fierce. So she's going with you -- to Africa?'

'That's the plan, but this shortfall might change things. I'm not sure really....'

'So you do more than just provide some funds?'

'I do some of the PR except the website which she does. That's boring but she does all the admin and I've got to say -- holds the whole thing together. Without her, Africa-Read-Write wouldn't function. She does so much, here and in Kembazi - but she isn't marvellous with people. I wouldn't employ her in our business -- but then she does get things done. She just batters down any resistance.'

'So you provide the funds and she spends it...?'

'Well, me and others. She coordinates. She works with the local people in the area where we've got the schools. That's a long way from the capital. She works hard - it's her life. And it's changed the lives of dozens of kids out there -- perhaps hundreds, especially girls.'

'Hundreds -- that's amazing.'

'It is amazing. I mean apart from this short-term problem, we've got three new secondary schools up and running - that's really something. Getting a tongue-lashing from Marion is nothing set against that.'

'It's fantastic Jill. I'd love to get more involved. It's so important.'

'And handle Marion? That's no fun. Anyway you are involved. You free me up to do the ARW stuff. Look Sadie, I've got to rush now and sort out some things...I'm forgetting everything today.'

Jill was still flustered, 'You're OK on your own here, aren't you.....'

And she collected up various papers and dashed away leaving me feeling that -- yes, I was becoming indispensible.

It was a lovely brisk evening and I decided to walk home to the flat. On the way I thought that I wanted

to do more than free Jill up. I wanted to get directly
involved. I had noted the comment about a boring
web site -- another one needing attention. Perhaps
this was a way in?

When I got back to the flat, Kyle was there
with his sister. It was Mel's turn to cook in my small
kitchen, so Kyle and I had a coffee in the living room.
I was still a bit high from thinking about Africa-Read-
Write and how much I'd love to be involved and
chatted on about it to Kyle. To my surprise, he was not
impressed.

'It's just a drop in the ocean, Sadie. What about
all the other millions of kids? They don't count I
suppose...'

'Of course they do, but it's a start. If it's only giving
education and choice to fifty girls, that's important to
each individual, isn't it?'

'What about the homeless folk in London -- and
the beggars? Have you never heard of -- charity
begins at home?'

'Of course I have -- that's important too. You've
got to get a balance.'

'Anyway I bet your boss'll soon get sick of wasting
this money....'

I was really surprised at this. Kyle and I had never
talked about these issues and I'd assumed we'd have
similar views -- but he was quite serious.

'No she won't. You don't even know her, Kyle....'

Mel brought in the food so we left it at that, but
the exchange with Kyle left me thinking. Why was I so
keen on Africa-Read-Write? Part of it was about Jill;
another was wanting to visit Africa again. I'd had a few
weeks in South Africa with an uncle and aunt before
going to college. But my main reason was because

I wanted to live in a better world, where everyone
has a chance. Kyle might think I was naive about the
problems of the world -- but I didn't care. I knew he's
been on package holidays but he hadn't travelled as
I had. It would have seemed pompous to Kyle, but I
saw myself as a citizen of the world.

62

10

At the end of the next day at work, as I was locking the outer door, I became aware of someone hovering on the pavement near me. It was Baz's friend, Eva. This was a surprise; I had warmed to this blowsy woman, despite her dreadful taste in men.

'Hello Sadie. Do you think I can have a quick word? Or are you rushing off?'

She seemed to expect rejection. We were standing almost exactly where Tariq had manhandled Baz into the car a few days previously. Did she know about that?

She was about my height in her high heels, too high for a person of her weight, too much makeup, stiff blond dyed hair, her podgy face was quite pretty for someone pushing on (at a guess) late forties. The overall effect was way over the top, but somehow I liked her all the more for it.

'Well...I've got five minutes. Do you want to go back into the gallery?'

'No -- I waited outside to check that Jill wasn't around.'

'Right -- but why?'

'There's a coffee bar over there. Can I buy you one? And a cake?'

'Eva, this sounds like bribery....'

'Oh no -- I just want a chat, that's all'.

This was clearly untrue but a coffee was tempting and I was curious.

We crossed the road and entered the local café. It was an old-fashioned place, with a welcoming young woman behind the bar and some tempting home-made cakes on display.

Eva giggled. 'I shouldn't but I can't resist one of those'.

We each chose a cake. Eva ordered the coffee, then I led the way towards the window seats so I could look at Gallery Elite over the road, but Eva stopped me.

She mouthed to me, 'This is private.'

She led me to a more discreet table where we settled ourselves, compared cakes and waited for our coffees. Then, with a sigh, she started.

'It's Baz. I was so grateful that you looked at his painting. We were both thrilled that you liked it. You won't believe how it's encouraged him.'

'I did like it. I was quite surprised by it, actually.'

I fished out my phone and got the photo of the painting up so we could both see it.

'I wasn't sure about the title -- Subconscious something, but the painting's bold and well integrated, quite exciting really.'

'Oh, that's wonderful. He's done a few more. I know Jill won't have them in the gallery, but they should be up somewhere...'

'I agree. You're right.'

'Oh Sadie, you don't know what a relief it is to hear you say that.'

I thought to myself -- do you know about his drunken collapse in the gallery? I didn't want to hurt or upset her, but how well did she know her boyfriend?

'Did he tell you about when he came to collect the painting?'

She read my tone of voice straight away. 'No – oh no. Don't tell me he was the worse for wear....'

'I'm afraid so..'

'How bad?'

'….you don't want to know.'

'Tell me the worst Sadie. I'm trying to help him fight it…'

'Well, to be honest, he collapsed on the gallery floor. He was out of it for a while. Jill's husband came to help get him home.'

'No! Oh Sadie, that's awful. I'm so sorry. Really. You shouldn't have to deal with that sort of thing…'

Eva got a little tearful. I felt sorry for her.

'When a gallery's open to the public, things happen. To be honest, I've seen far worse'.

'Have you? Really?'

It wasn't true but I wanted to soften the blow. 'Oh yes, collapses, even deaths…' More lies. 'Is he often in that condition?'

'Not that often. I've seen him -- well, falling over -- a few times, especially when he gets stressed. It was the painting. He was worried about what you'd say. If he has a few hours to fill in, he drinks…I'm trying to help him and we're getting there, slowly, but I'm not with him all the time and he's up and down. He goes to Alcoholics Anonymous. That helps.'

'Right.'

'But if he could make progress with his painting, that would be a life-saver. Of course, that's where the family problems come in -- with Jill and the father….'

'When you say *make progress*, do you mean selling?'

'Yes, isn't that what it's all about?'

'Many people get pleasure just by doing their art, maybe displaying it on the web or local amateur exhibitions. I mean Baz has got a day job, hasn't he?'

'He's in property, but I'm frightened he'll turn up drunk and wreck that. There've been some near scrapes. Does Jill know about -- being drunk in the gallery?'

'I haven't told her, but Tariq might have. And Sean was around at Baz's flat...'

'She'll know all about it then. Another nail in his coffin. That's why I wanted to talk to you Sadie.'

My heart sank. I was being recruited to help her save Baz.

'I knew something had happened. I picked that up from him. For a start, why should you and Tariq come to the flat and not even come in to see his other paintings?'

'I see. He didn't tell you?'

'Sometimes he doesn't remember these things -- or doesn't choose to.'

'Baz wanted me to come in but Sean stopped him and almost closed the door in our face.'

'Sean's bossy. He's gay, you know. I wouldn't want to cross him. Baz thinks he's marvellous but if he's at Baz's flat, I know my place – I'm the housemaid. I sometimes think I'm stupid putting up with it. You'd never do that, would you Sadie. You're too smart.'

'I don't know. Sometimes it's clever just to play along with other people's little games.'

I recalled the strange tensions when we delivered Baz to his flat.

I wondered how much she knew and asked, 'Are Tariq and Sean buddies?'

'They work together, don't they? And doesn't Sean treat Tariq's back, massage treatment I think. I don't really know.'

'Right. And does Baz work with Sean sometimes?'

'Well, I'm not supposed to say anything about

that. It's all hush-hush. I've probably said too much.
Baz really wants to get involved in the family business
and I think Sean might help him a bit -- but what do
I know? It might or might not happen. What I want
to do is to help Baz get over his alcohol thing -- and
his painting distracts him. He loves it. That's why I'm
asking your advice. What can we do?'

I had to be careful. I liked Eva but was not going
to take on Baz or his art.
'Selling painting is tough especially when money
is tight. To be blunt, if he's only doing it for cash, if
there's no reward in the activity itself, he ought to find
something else.'
'Oh, he really enjoys his painting. He spends
hours doing it'.
'Well on the positive side, there are several selling
sites on the web. He ought to take a look at those.
Some are really good.'
'Really. I'll tell him that. Which sites?'
'Well look, give me your email address and I'll
send you some to look at.'
'Shall I write it on this serviette?'
'OK right. Look, I've got to get home now. I'm
cooking tonight...'

That seemed to settle it for her, or at least she
saw that she was going to get nothing more from me,
so she didn't ask. We parted as friends -- or at least
as allies against the mad world.

11

'Hi Sadie -- come right up. Flat 25.'

Despite Tariq's advice, I wanted to know more about Sean. The guy intrigued me – and I admit to finding him attractive – back then. Out of the blue, he rang me and said he had some time if I wanted to do some web stuff, and his flatmate was going out. I didn't think I was taking any risks. I can look after myself anyway -- and Sean wouldn't do anything stupid with a colleague, would he?

He opened the door with a big smile. 'Hi Sadie. Good to see you.'

No handshake or kiss or anything -- which was fine by me. He looked great -- dressed as if he had just returned from a run, but fresh and with some distant man-perfume.

'I'm just making coffee, thought we'd have a chat first about what you know -- what you want.....see if we have the same agenda.'

'OK -- that sounds fine.'

He glided into the kitchen which gave me a chance to look around. A fair sized living room. No art. Climbing and travel posters, an exercise machine, a laptop plugged into a large monitor, a cosy sofa in front of a large TV, switched on but muted -- rugby. All very masculine.

Then, to my utter astonishment, Kyle walked in. He came from a side room, a bedroom perhaps? We gaped at each other then he put a finger to his lips. What was Mel's brother doing here? He was in smart jeans and tee-shirt, his spiky hair well oiled -- but he looked pale, different from his usual chirpy self. I was amazed at meeting him here, and he looked completely thrown.

We both looked towards the kitchen where a kettle was boiling.

He whispered, 'Sadie! What the hell are you doing here?'

I whispered back, 'The web site -- what about you?'

'You aren't with....' -- and he nodded towards the kitchen. What on earth was he thinking?

'We work together -- Kyle, what's up? Are you..... do you live here?'

He half nodded. Glancing towards the kitchen he whispered, 'It's not working out -- it's getting impossible. Don't tell Mel. OK?'

'Alright -- if you say so....'

Sean swept in with two mugs of coffee.

'You still here Kyle? I thought you'd be off by now....'

'Just going -- on my way....bye...'

And he left -- with barely a look in my direction. And I thought I knew him.

Sean and I sat down with our coffees and faced each other.

'So you met our Kyle?'

I thought - play dumb. 'That guy? Does he live here?'

'He's in the spare room -- helps with the mortgage. What did he say?'

'Oh nothing -- I thought I'd seen him around, that's all.'

'Well if you go to the Park Tavern round the corner, he's behind the bar.'

'Oh -- that's it. I've probably seen him there.'

My mind was brimming with questions, but Kyle's whispered 'it's not working out' and Sean's 'helps with the mortgage', kept me silent.

'OK, Sadie. So -- sounds like you want to take over my web job? According to Jill....'

I snorted, 'No chance. I haven't even got a permanent job myself -- anyway I'm into art not computers, well art promotion.'

' Ah -- so it's the content you want to get your mits on!'

'I've got a few thoughts but I'm here to learn. And I haven't that much experience. I mean, do you do the content yourself, as well as the -- technical stuff?'

'You've got to blame Jill for most of that. She gives me content. I add a bit of fun -- and I do some tweaking when she goes over the top.'

'Right. And is that a lot of tweaking?'

'No -- but frankly she's got no idea and then she likes to smuggle in stuff about Africa, little bits and pieces. I keep telling her it doesn't make sense. What do you think?'

'You mean it doesn't make sense on this particular website. ...'

'You've got it. You know she's obsessed with Africa, don't you ...'

'Is she? You mean with girls' education?'

'Sure. All that stuff.'

'But it's good, what she's doing. I mean when you think of girls marrying young and having loads of kids before they're even grown-up. Surely that's good.'

'Oh come on, Sadie. It's a drop in the ocean...'

That was the phrase Kyle had used. Of course, if they share a flat, live together perhaps, they're going to talk -- and the older man will influence the younger.

I played ignorant, 'I suppose so...'

'It's all about Jill you know -- making herself feel better about her lifestyle.'

I was stunned -- marvellous Jill? I suppose my face showed it.

He gave me a knowing smile, 'I'm beginning to think you're another lost cause. I never took you for Saint Sadie...'

'For heaven's sake, I'm no saint. I can promise you that.'

'Just joking.....so you're no saint?'

'Right. But there are different ways of looking at these things, you know. I think we should do some web stuff now, because I don't think we're going to agree about Africa.'

He shrugged, 'OK, OK -- whatever....'

He got up and led the way over to the computer. It was a laptop with a large monitor plugged in. All the kit was squeezed into a corner so the two of us had to sit rather closely -- unavoidably it seemed.

'OK. Let's start here -- see what you make of this...'

He showed me one or two of the features and the code behind them.

'Look at this – look at this. This is so clever...' There was a picture of the outside of our gallery with small stars that floated out of the door.

'Now watch!' He switched to the code, changed some number, switched back to the picture – now there were loads of large stars moving much faster. To me any stars at all were completely inappropriate – but he was so thrilled, and I couldn't help admiring his expertise.

Also, I was starting to be distracted by his physical proximity. I tried to focus on the editing screen -- but was only aware of the warmth of his leg -- and its slight twitching movement. Stop, I said to myself and edged away from him -- but there was no room.

I tried to focus, 'So this is where you – edit the code....'

'Yeess -- this is where it all happens...'

To my alarm, my rational self started melting away. I can say that now -- it was like an automatic reaction. Hormones and stuff. My breathing was becoming shallow -- would he notice? The screen was melting before my eyes. I stopped being myself.

'We call this -- the editing screen -- well sometimes....'

His hand brushed against my upper leg then slid across to adjust his arousal.

He said slowly, 'I think I'm starting to talk garbage....what about you....'

I was taking short breaths, 'I don't know -- I'm trying to concentrate...'

He slid his office chair back then slowly turned towards me, adjusting his clothes. He grabbed my hand and pulled it on to him. He started using my hand.

After a few moments, I pulled away and jumped up. Then I remember scuttling to what looked like the bathroom -- and locked the door. What a stupid situation to get into – I'm not having sex with anybody just because they're attractive – and what of him and Kyle?.

Suddenly my head was filled with Jill and little Harry. What the hell was I doing? I felt humiliated, yet nothing much had happened -- and he was as much to blame as me. Then I started becoming myself again -- the rational Sadie. I needed to get out of this place.

I pulled myself together, washed my hands. In the mirror I looked woeful. A forced smile got a grimace in return. A minute more to sort myself out -- then I had to face him again. I felt so foolish.

I forced herself to be tall, composed -- and walked back into the living room. He was tapping away at the keyboard.

'Oh hi! You OK?'

'No, but I'll survive.....'

'Good -- to be very honest Sadie' -- he beamed a self-satisfied smile at me, 'We could have a great time together...'

'Really! Well, to be very honest with you Sean, that's the last thing I need right now...'

He laughed. 'Sadie, you don't have to pretend. It was obvious..'

My voice started rising, 'You don't know me Sean -- and you're definitely not getting the chance.'

He looked surprised and slightly hurt, 'Right -- whatever...so....let's some web stuff? Come on. Look, I'm sorry -- that was just a physical thing -- these things happen. We'll forget about it -- it never happened! Deleted -- OK?'

'No, not deleted -- and I can't just switch into the web stuff.'

'No worries -- have another coffee first....a drink?'

'No. I'm going -- we can do the web another time -- in the office at work or somewhere...'

'OK, OK Sadie. Whatever -- I'm not exactly short of things to do – or people to help me out for that matter....'

I moved awkwardly towards the flat door, trying to retain a fragment of dignity.

I opened the door and half turned, 'Right. Bye then.' He followed me to the door, but at a distance.

'Bye Sadie -- and remember.....' I paused at the top of the stairs. 'Don't get too deep into the Africa thing. It's not going to last -- I can promise you. Jill's an obsessive, then she flips into something else -- you just watch. But keep that to yourself. By the way, the lift's that way.'

That knowing smile!

'I'll use the stairs, thank you.'

Well that was a disaster. Beautiful people can be a menace and Sean had a weird sort of beauty, but it was only on the outside. It was so humiliating to have him say 'you don't have to pretend, it was obvious'.

Who might he tell that it was so 'obvious' and what might he say? Jill – no! Kyle? As far as Sean's concerned Kyle and I don't know each other – but Kyle would quiz him, would bring it up casually. Should I email Sean to demand that he keeps silent? No, that could backfire – just do nothing.

Anyway why was I so worked up about it? A man and a woman get the hots for each other, then one of them calls a halt before things go too far. That's not so special. But then this was different -- the man might be close to a younger man who was my best friend's brother and who was my sort-of boyfriend. What a mess. I thought of Eva telling me Sean was gay and I suddenly felt a bit hysterical.

12

The day after my encounter with Sean, and a bad night's sleep, I sat at the receptionist's desk in the empty gallery, trying to forget about it and him. I knew I was going to be haunted by questions about who Sean might tell and other questions about Kyle. Then Jill rang my mobile and asked some new ones which completely took over.

'Is that you Sadie?'

'Yes. Hi Jill.'

'Listen -- have you got a passport?'

'Yes.'

She sounded upset, even manic. 'Do you want a trip to Africa?'

'Well -- yes, I'd love it. But how?'

'Tariq's ill. I can't leave him. He's in a bad state.'

'Right. But you're not going till next week. He might recover...'

'I'm not taking any risks. Sadie, I can't leave Harry with him. I've never seen him so low. The pills don't seem to touch it.'

'Oh Jill, I'm so sorry. Can't I look after Harry or something?'

She was on the verge of tears, 'That's sweet of you Sadie, but I need to stay with Tariq and keep Harry safe. I don't mean Harry's in any danger, but sometimes Tariq can't even wake up. So I've got to be there for them both....'

I can't pretend I wasn't thrilled but I hid that, 'Right. I understand.'

'You go to Africa with Marion. It won't be a bed of roses, I promise you that. You'll just be fetching and carrying for her.'

'I can do that, Jill. Is that next week?'

'Can you manage that?'

'Well yes, if you can spare me from here….'

I was fantastically excited. I'd had that holiday with my uncle and aunt (my mother's sister) in Cape Town and might have flown over Kembazi in the dark but knew almost nothing about it. I had looked at Marion's ARW website and seen a few small photos of the three schools, the staff and the pupils.

Jill wanted to brief me on the trip right away but could not leave Tariq. Harry was at play school. I closed the gallery early and went to their home. When I got there, Tariq was in bed. Jill and I sat down with her Kembazi file.

We listed the things I had to do. The most urgent were to get a visa from the High Commission and to get a yellow fever jab. The transfer of air ticket and health insurance from Jill to me needed to be fixed and Jill knew how to arrange these; she told me exactly what to do and gave me cash for the visa and jab.

Then she gave me maps of Kembazi northern region where the schools were, details of the school staff, especially Joseph, the Head of the school where we were to be based, information about ARW, some background papers.

'Marion will probably give you loads more stuff, knowing her.'

'Right. Does she know you're not going?'

'Not yet. I've been putting that off, after our last set-to. I'll ring her this evening. She won't like it but I'm not giving her any choice.'

From Jill's house, I set off straight back to the flat to tell Mel the news of my trip. I knew she'd be pleased for me. Then I remembered that Kyle was likely to be there. I didn't want to meet him and this would be the first time since being at Sean's. I just felt angry with him. Seeing him like that in Sean's flat made him seem like a different person. Maybe he really was Sean's boyfriend or something, rather than just a lodger. I couldn't think romantically about him anymore. What had happened between Sean and me, made it worse. Had I almost had sex with Kyle's lover? I felt churned up. I prayed that Kyle knew nothing of what had happened between Sean and me. I couldn't bear that, and I had no idea how Sean might spin it.

I seriously thought about ringing Mel and saying I had to go to Walter's, but she was cooking and she always took a lot of trouble. I had to face Kyle one day even if I couldn't vent my anger when Mel was around.

When I arrived at the flat, Kyle winked at me behind Mel's back and put his fingers to his lips. So I wasn't to mention our meeting at Sean's flat? Did he want me to pretend it hadn't happened? He'd said 'don't tell Mel' at Sean's place and I'd agreed, but I guess he was still worried. Perhaps this was about Kyle coming out to his family? Mel wouldn't be fussed, that's for sure. She's like me about gay stuff.

She was cooking. Kyle and I could have had a private word before the meal, but neither of us made any move to do that. I went to my room then Mel called me for the meal -- pasta with a great sauce. This time Kyle did not quiz me about what I was up to, and we both tried to act normal though I think Mel guessed that something was up.

Then I told them my big news -- about the trip.

Mel was thrilled for me, 'You lucky thing. It'll be fabulous. I'm so envious….when do you go?'

Kyle was muted but curious, 'Are you going in place of your boss? So why's that?'

'Her partner's ill. He needs looking after -- and they've a little boy…'

Kyle went silent. Mel plied me for more detail. I said to myself, shut up about Jill's private affairs in front of Kyle. So I told them some stuff about the Kembazi trip. Then Kyle did the dishes and the three of us watched a DVD.

Next morning, I made my way to the entrance of the Kembazi High Commission. The passport and visa office gave me a first taste of Kembazi people. After a thirty minute queue, I handed in my application form, passport and the fee, then was marooned for another hour and a half with about seventy other people in a waiting room. It wasn't too bad because I could chat with my neighbours. Most of them were Kembazi people. I really enjoyed it; they were very friendly and open, people of all ages. A number of children were getting to know one another, playing around.

A small family of three were next to me. The man was doing a further degree in Environmental Science. He asked me why I was here and I explained about ARW.

'Oh, I've heard of that project. It's very good.'

His wife said, 'I read that these schools only have girl pupils. Is that right?'

I said, 'I think there are boys as well. But I have heard that quite young girls start having children very young, then they have no choice about their future.'

'Some start young, in the country areas. It's custom. Not in the city where we come from.'

The man said, 'But many people think the traditional ways are best. Like my parents, who find it bad that we only have one child. My wife is a nurse. She has a good job here.'

Then we had a very lively discussion about the relative advantages of modern and traditional ways. The three of us mostly agreed. They thought that traditional ways would not alter for generations in the country areas.

Then a hatch opened and everyone rushed forward. Those with the sharpest elbows got to collect their documents first. I joined the scrum and was far from last..

I met Marion in the gallery office. Jill had said she would also be there but Tariq had a bad turn, so there were only the two of us. Marion sat down opposite me in what felt like confrontation mode -- and launched into complaints.

'This is very unsatisfactory, Jill not appearing today, especially given the difficulties of this particular visit. I would have thought she could have made the effort.'

'Her partner's illness is unpredictable. That's all.'

'Like her control over her finances it seems...has she told you about that?'

'Yes. She mentioned that.'

'I dread to think what our colleagues in Kembazi will say...'

'We'll have to do the best we can, use all our skills.'

'Humph. You haven't met them.'

After more complaints, she calmed down. I tried to be constructive.

'So do I take notes at your meetings? What is the most useful thing for me to do?'

This struck a better tone and we talked through what was likely to happen in our short visit. Then she moved into complaints mode again.

'I must say that Jill dropping out like this is very unhelpful. You have so little experience.'

I was being put in my place again and I'd had enough. I was not going to have this adventure overlaid by moaning and mild humiliation.

'Marion, this is not my first time in Africa.'

'Really? But you've never been to Kembazi surely?...'

'No but I was in South Africa.'

'Ah well, there you are -- a very different place.'

I had to take more control. I'm not marvellous in conflict situations but I had to assert myself or this was going to go on and on.

I looked at her full in the face and said sharply, 'Of course it is. But if you keep treating me like a total innocent, we aren't going to get on. I mean you don't know anything about me.'

Even I was surprised for I'm not often like that. Marion just stared at me. She was not accustomed to people holding a mirror up to her.

'I see. Well I'm sure you're not totally innocent Sadie, whatever that may mean, but you are coming as my assistant.'

'But not as your slave or clone -- and we do need to get on...'

'Of course we do.'

'Marion, would you rather I didn't come? Because that's the impression you're giving.'

She paused. 'Well I definitely need someone
to help me. It would be difficult on my own and
especially with the changes in the financial situation.
I don't know how they will react out there. I'm worried
about it....'

'So is that a yes or a no?'

She paused again and hung her head a little,
'I'm sorry if I gave you the wrong impression, Sadie. I
know I'm inclined to be blunt. That's just me.'

'Right. And....'

'I would rather you came -- and of course we must
get on with each other. We have to.'

'Good. That's fine then. Now is there anything
else you need to tell me?'

Another pause and an appraising look, 'I believe
I've covered everything.'

I closed up my notepad and stood up. 'That's fine.
I'll see you at 9:30 on Tuesday in Terminal 3 at the
Kembazi check-in. Shall I see you out?'

Marion understood I was not her doormat. She
collected her papers and said, 'I think I know the way,
thank you.'

13

The next few days were all manic preparation. Then after what seemed a blink, I was with Marion, waiting to board an overnight flight from London to Kembazi international airport. She was there before me, looking anxious. We checked in, passed through security then found a coffee bar to sit. She was soon justifying the arrangements again but it bothered me less, as I knew I could stand up to her.

'The truth is that when Jill backed out, I couldn't get a refund on the ticket, so there was no point in just wasting it. And I do need someone to help me. This is not going to be all fun. You know that, don't you, Sadie?'

'Marion, for me, this is fun. And apart from that, I'm strongly committed to working on the project and helping you as best I can.'

'Oh well, that's something I suppose. I admire your high spirits of course. I think I may have been like that when I was younger.'

It was difficult to imagine the younger Marion before she became this bossy pedant. But I knew I could cope with her -- and it was nothing compared with being married off at fifteen and having loads of kids.

The whole journey completely blew my mind. It had been years since that stay in South Africa with my aunt and uncle. This was so different. The passengers waiting in the departure lounge were very similar to the crowd renewing their passports -- colourful,

good-humoured, friendly. Some of the children were
fractious as it was way past their bed-time. There was
a smattering of Europeans, like Marion and myself.
Eventually we were crammed into our economy seats
and got ready for the seven-hour overnight flight from
the UK. When we reached cruising height, supper
was served and we battled with plastic to access
some bland chicken and veg. We both had some
wine. I clinked Marion's glass and said 'bon voyage'.

She said, 'To be honest Sadie, I am not expecting
this voyage to be very bon at all, but we can always
hope.' For Marion, this was a joke. Things were
looking up...

I didn't sleep much from excitement. Marion
dozed off and kept slumping forward. I followed our
progress on the screen map, across the Alps, the
Mediterranean, Algeria and the Sahara -- then I must
have fallen asleep because next we were descending
to the Kembazi capital. I peered out at the patchy
green landscape, quite mountainous, coming closer
and closer.

Getting out of the plane at six am in the tropics,
it was still cool. The sun had not risen. The air was a
heady mixture of exotic fragrance and aero fuel. Dawn
bird calls from the airport perimeter were raucous.
Security and customs passed in a dazed blur. Marion
knew her way around and soon we were in the small
departure lounge for internal flights. We had a two
hour wait so I tried to doze before the short flight to
the second city. There we were to be met by Joseph,
the head teacher of the school where we were
staying.

Walking from the airport building across to the
small plane was a shock. I was a bit robotic with
tiredness. The now dazzling brilliance of the sun and

the treacly humidity had me blinking the sweat from my eyes. We were much nearer the equator than Cape Town, where I'd been on my first Africa trip.

The small propeller plane only had about twenty seats and was far from full. We were welcomed on board by a bubbly flight assistant and shown into the second row, with a good view of the pilot in the open cabin. We quickly worked out how to direct some cool air on to our faces. The takeoff was extremely noisy.

It was a thirty or forty minute flight from the capital to the second city. I followed the landscape below, from the small international airport, over the outer city areas. They looked like impoverished, shanty towns, then some agricultural areas interspersed with scrubland -- then the reverse as we approached the second city airport.

Getting out of the plane was like walking into cotton wool. I was disorientated by all the new images, the humidity and tiredness. My head clammed up. I found I could hardly even form words.

Head teacher Joseph was waiting for us in the small regional airport. He had two children with him, a boy and a girl aged around six. He was a nice guy in his forties, bearded, rather good looking, heavily built, very black. He greeted Marion with respect, shook both of our hands. He obviously knew who I was. He seemed friendly, clearheaded and had pretty good English. The children were shy and shook our hands with eyes lowered. He led us out to a jeep. I was in the back with the luggage and the kids. The younger one, the boy, was in the middle. It was a bit crowded and I could hardly speak at that stage but no one seemed bothered. I guess Joseph was used to new arrivals being like zombies. He chatted with

Marion about our journey as we passed through the town. Away from the centre, houses became more bedraggled. Poverty was written on the faces of many of the people.

We were soon on to unmade country roads. It was bumpy and noisy but I didn't care – I was in Africa. Joseph and Marion started talking more seriously.

'So how is Jill? She herself is not ill?'

'Jill is well. It's her husband who is ill and they have a little boy.'

'That's a problem, when the woman works and then something goes wrong. I know things are different in UK but sometimes the old ways are best. Or to not get married at all, like you Marion? Your husband is not going to get ill.'

I think that was meant to be a joke but Marion said icily, 'That's true Joseph, but we're not here to talk about my personal circumstances.'

' Sorry Marion. I've offended you -- again.' Joseph seemed to have a chuckle in his voice as he said this.

'I'm not offended Joseph.' Her tone of voice gave the lie to that. 'It's just that my personal circumstances are none of your business. Now if we must talk, please let's talk about school matters.'

After a few minutes of noisy bouncing around with no conversation at all, Marion said, 'Joseph, I'm afraid I've some bad news...'

'Most news is bad news Marion. I'm used to it.'

'Joseph, this is serious. It's the finances'.

'Ah – yes. I had a long email from Jill – no extra funds available at present. She was very apologetic.'

'Oh, so you know already. Yes, it is very bad news.'

'Not so bad Marion. More time for careful planning, less time for mistakes. That's what I told Jill.'

'But we've done all the planning Joseph. We were ready to build...'

'Were we? I think that here we are more flexible. Life is always full of surprises.'

Marion was silenced by this homespun common sense. I realised that Joseph had probably seen more of life than Marion or I could conceive. He was unperturbed by her or her news.

It was about two hour's journey from the town to the school and the road was worse than anything I've ever experienced. It was an unmade dirt track. The vehicle suspension was hard so that at times Joseph's children and I were thrown against one another. The little boy reminded me of Harry. I put my arm around his shoulder to stabilise us both but we were still thrown all over the place. At the same time it was like a dream. I kept saying to myself -- 'I'm in Africa, on an adventure' -- as I bounced up and down with a head full of cotton wool and sweating in the humidity.

The school was on the edge of a small village in a fenced off area about the size of a football pitch. It was very functional. I'd seen photos of the breezeblock building with the residential blocks tucked behind. At one side was a small bungalow, which I guessed was where Joseph and his family lived. Around twenty pupils came out to greet us. It was late afternoon so they weren't in school uniform. What a lively, colourful bunch, with huge smiles and waves. After a long journey, it was heart warming to have such a welcome.

They gathered around the jeep and called out,

'Welcome Madam Marion. Welcome Marion's friend.'

Joseph said, 'Madam Jill is not able to come this time as her family is ill.'

One of the boys said, 'That's bad....we hope the family recover very soon'.

'So -- Madam Sadie has come in her place.'

They looked at me with much interest and smiles.

I smiled back and tried to say, 'Hello everyone'. I'm not sure any words came out.

We climbed out of the jeep and my young backseat companions took me by the hand, one on each side, and led me through the small crowd of pupils towards Joseph's bungalow. The young children, petted and patted as they went by, were obvious favourites. I was still barely capable of speech so it was good being led in this way. Marion had told me we would be fed at Joseph's house. At the door were three people who I guessed were Joseph's wife and his other two children.

Joseph introduced me to Augusta, his wife, then to Alpha, a fine looking boy almost as tall as me -- and three year old Doris. We were led into the living room, very plain and functional by European standards, and were asked to sit at the table, all eight of us. Augusta wore a bright orange dress and a red head scarf and had a warm affectionate manner.

She had prepared a substantial meal:- chicken and vegetable stew with rice. She started by ladling out a good helping of stew for Marion, Joseph and myself, urged us to help ourselves to rice. Augusta then turned to her children and finally herself. Alpha poured out fruit juice for all of us. Later there were cake and biscuits. They made Marion and me very welcome.

Joseph said to me, 'Augusta's the clever one you

know. She teaches Maths in the school...'

Marion added, 'Don't you teach English as well to the older pupils?'

'Yes, I do both, as well as looking after this family.'

I was in awe of her doing what sounded like two full-time jobs -- and I was getting my speech back after the lack of sleep and the drama of the journey.

'How do you manage it all?'

'I have a very busy life -- but I'm happy, thank the Lord. I have lots of help. Now excuse me Sadie, but I must have a word with Isac. Isac, will you please stop staring at Madam Sadie. It's rude.'

'But she's my friend. We sat together in the jeep.'

Lucee, the seven your old, burst in, 'Me too. She's my friend as well. Just because you were next to her...'

Alpha, the oldest, said, 'I wanted to come to meet the two madams. It's not fair. I had to do boring chores.'

Joseph took on his head master's voice. 'That's enough children. You can all be friends with Madam Sadie -- and she has no favourites.'

Augusta added, 'I have to tell you all that Alpha made a lovely job in the chicken house. The birds all looked very happy and clean.'

After the meal, Augusta took me to my small bedroom in a small visitors' rest house next to her bungalow. It was simple but perfect for my needs.

I looked at the bed and said, 'Augusta, do you mind if I lie down for a little while?'

'You mean right now?'

'I'm completely jiggered -- I mean exhausted.'

'You lie down and rest Sadie. I'm sure Marion and Joseph have lots to talk about. Later, if you want,

Joseph will take you to meet some of the pupils.'

I woke up more than an hour later with a clear
head and a feeling of intense excitement. I drew back
the bright yellow curtains to see the jeep parked in
the unpaved entrance area. The school, the dorms
and the bungalows formed three sides. Beyond was a
densely wooded area, now dark against the low sun,
forbidding. I could see how this chunk of civilisation
had been hacked out of raw nature which had to be
held back.

I joined the others at Joseph's house. He took
me straight out again to the dormitory area as several
girls had been waiting to show me around, while I'd
been sleeping. They were outside their dorm by the
sinks they used for cleaning clothes, with clothes
lines of flapping washing. They were a group of five
very friendly young women, in jeans and a variety of
colourful tops. At this point they all looked the same
to me, but that would change. Anyway I started by
explaining why I had been so tired. Then they quizzed
me about the journey. I think their ages were around
fifteen or sixteen. They wanted to show me their
accommodation -- basic, very clean -- and the girls
themselves looked very clean, despite the humidity.
They showed me the small farm where their food was
grown and animals lived. They were as curious about
me as I was about them.

Suzan and Olivette were the most confident and
open of the girls. They told me they came from the
same village a few miles away and they wanted to
be teachers. They did not want to marry for several
years and to have no more than two children;
this was almost unheard of locally. They seemed
worldly wise and determined to avoid alcohol and its

consequences.

After they had told me about their lives and ambitions, Olivette said, 'Madam, can I ask you a question?'

'Yes, go ahead, but there's no need to call me Madam. My name is Sadie.'

'Sadie, that is a nice name. I have never heard it before. My question is -- are you married?'

'No. I haven't met anyone I want to marry yet. And I'm in no hurry.'

Suzan was worried by my answer, 'Madam Sadie, you ought to hurry. Truly you ought. You are older than us and it will become too late. Nobody will have you.'

'Well in my country women often marry quite late. Even in their thirties they can marry and have children. Even later they can marry and have no children. It's their choice.'

They were surprised by my answer, looking at each other, discreetly rolling their eyes. They wanted freedom from the old oppressions, but I seemed to have gone beyond all reason.

Olivette said, 'Madam Sadie, is Madam Marion married?'

I searched for a diplomatic answer, 'I don't think so. She's devoted her life to getting more education for people like you...'

Suzan said, 'We are very grateful to her. She is like a nun for education. Some of us are Christians in this school so we can understand her. Sadie, are you a Christian or a Muslim?'

'Well to be honest, neither...one day I think I might become a Buddhist.'

This prompted great surprise. How could I not be one or the other? We had a discussion about religions

-- and they listened with interest to my stories of the different lives people lead in Britain. They were a rapt audience. I felt that I was a window on the world outside. I'd never fully understood how lucky we are in Britain, well in most of Europe really, how we just take as our rights all the wealth and freedom we have.

The next two days were a bit of a haze. We visited the site of the possible new school and worked on the action plan for when funds eventually appeared. Then there were the finances of the existing three schools, pupil numbers and loads of linked detail to consider. I was Marion's secretary, holding her documents, taking notes of key points, then transcribing these into Marion's laptop. With the heat and humidity, I was less efficient than I usually am. I was determined to muddle through and Marion seemed satisfied.

In the evenings, we joined Joseph, Augusta and their family for a meal. Later, after the younger children had gone to bed, I helped Augusta with the dishes. Then we drank tea and told tales to one another about the madness of the world. I was soon fighting with sleep and I was relieved to see Marion's head fall forward now and then -- so on our final day, it was early to bed.

Next day, after a rushed breakfast, we were suddenly hugging Joseph's family goodbye and waving to the pupils, Suzan and Olivette among them. Leaving was a wrench. Even after this short stay I felt a surge of emotion. Joseph, Augusta and their children had been so welcoming -- and as for the school pupils, they were delightful. I don't often get weepy but I really had to swallow hard. It wasn't just the people, it was the great importance of this project in transforming lives; to me this was a massive experience.

In the jeep on the journey back to the regional airport, without the children this time and more awake, I was able to look closely at the hilly landscape and occasional villages. Joseph dropped us at the departure entrance; he had to get back to his classes. I enjoyed the short flight to the capital, armed now with some knowledge and a growing affection towards the country and its people.

In the capital airport, we had two hours wait. Marion was back on wi-fi so could access her emails. I wondered around the airport, then just sat down a little away from Marion. We had got on reasonably well. Her bossiness towards me had softened. She did not have to hold me at bay as she did with Jill.

For me, it had been a great adventure. I was involved in giving young people new opportunities. I was determined to get more and more involved in the future.

14

It was a few days before I settled into normal life again. On the second day back, there was a feedback session with Marion and Jill. They now both accepted me as a junior team member and listened to my views. True it was mostly Jill who asked me what I thought and Marion who referred to executive decisions, but I felt my presence helped. At least they weren't squabbling. I was ready to step in with Joseph's view of working with events you can't change, and Marion was less pedantic than previously.

'Joseph was of course immensely disappointed at the news.'

I couldn't let this pass. 'Was he? I thought he took it all in his stride. He seemed quite laid back about it.'

'Ah but you only saw the surface of things. Remember I've known him for years. In any case Jill, you'd messaged him before we got there so he had time to prepare himself.'

Jill said, 'Joseph always says what he thinks. He's not out to hurt anybody but he calls a spade a spade.'

I had to intercept this struggle over who understands Joseph best.

'What he said was -- more time for careful planning, less time for mistakes. So, we are where we are as far as the finances are concerned. Now we need to look to the future.'

Jill said, 'You're right Sadie. You're beginning to sound like Joseph.'

Marion said nothing and looked grim, but she didn't pursue the matter. At least she didn't say --

Sadie dear, you're very young. Also I noticed that she quite often adopted my viewpoint as if it was her own original idea, which was both irritating and flattering.

Jill invited me round late one evening, after Tariq had gone to bed, where he was spending half of his life. She wanted to soak up all of my images of the trip. She was fond of Joseph and his family – and knew Suzan and Olivette. Reliving my trip was great. Jill had a wider perspective than Marion and had some fascinating stories about the development of the school and of the people.

Next day, after all of these excitements, I was back in the gallery alone, and the hollow nature of my job bore down on me. I was getting really frustrated as my talents were being wasted. I wanted something different to happen in my life. I was emailing my friend Beth, who had a job in Brussels, and I was actually asking her about jobs over there. I sent this off and soon after, the phone rang in the office; I thought -- it's Beth. Brussels.

'Gallery Elite -- how can I help you?'

There was a long pause, a grunt, then, 'Sadie, is that you? It's Walter here…'

'Grandfather! Is everything alright?'

'Not too bad darling. I've had another of those funny turns with my heart. They've brought me into hospital…'

He sounded very low.

'Oh Grandfather - how are you? Was it very bad?'

'More or less the same as last time - a pain in the chest - I pressed the panic button thingy and somebody came, eventually, with some oxygen and I've ended up here. The same bed as last time.'

'Shall I close the gallery and come round? Jill won't mind.'

'Come this evening, darling. I'll be fine till then.'

'Are you sure? Whatever suits you.'

'Visiting starts at six. And can you pick up some stuff from the flat - my wallet and toothbrush. And some clean underclothes for tomorrow. Sorry about this my dear…'

'It's fine - I'll get them.'

'Feed the cat. Oh and let Alice know. Leave her a note…she's not in today. Darling, I hate to impose on you…'

'Really Grandfather - it's nothing, it's a pleasure to look after you. And after all you've done for me…..but not just for that reason.'

At the flat, I soon collected the items Walter needed. Freud the cat was unused to being alone so I took her on my lap and petted her for a few minutes. I saw the answer-phone flashing and thought I ought to check for anything urgent. There were two messages, one new, one old. The new was a cold call; I deleted that. The old message was a man on a poor line, sounded like an echoing mobile.

As I listened, I froze, ' Alright Mr Alexander, you've got ten days to transfer the cash into the account I gave you, then we'll deliver. And if the transfer doesn't happen, you're going to get a nasty surprise.'

It was threatening, menacing. Not Grandfather's world at all. I braced myself to listen again.

' Alright Mr Alexander, you've got ten days to transfer the cash into the account I gave you, then we'll deliver. And if the transfer doesn't happen, you're going to get a nasty surprise.' Long bleep -- message ended.

I was stunned. A wrong number? No, the guy said Mr Alexander. I'd had hints of my Grandfather's darker side, but this sounded diabolical. I was scared. I tried to calm myself and think out what I should do.

Should I tell Walter about the call? It was an old call so he'd already heard it. He'd be upset, embarrassed, so what was I to do?

I wanted to just delete the message and purge it from existence, but it was there, gnawing away. I played it one further time -- and this time I recorded the message on my mobile, then deleted it from the answer phone. Too late, I realised he would know someone had listened to it. By this time, I could chant the message from memory, then I realised that 'the account I gave you' meant earlier contacts. What had my Grandfather got into? Had this message triggered the heart attack?

In the hospital, I was shown to the same private room as during the previous heart episode. Walter was wired up to various monitors and was asleep. I came in quietly, thinking that either this could be a deeply troubling meeting -- or else I could pretend I hadn't heard the message. I looked at his sleeping face, a face I loved, even though now grey, with flesh hanging in folds. This was the second episode in a year and I knew he was beginning to go downhill. I felt strongly that if he discovered that I had heard the message, it might be a great blow, even fatal. I must protect him, but I had to do something.

I took my Grandfather's hand and stroked it gently until he woke up. Then we had a discussion about his symptoms, the paramedics, the cat, and when he would come out, the next day at earliest. He sounded depressed, his speech was slow, he was unhappy. My heart went out to him. I held back from questioning him about whether anything was troubling him.

I couldn't admit to Walter that I knew about the call until he was out of danger. I had deleted the message but at least I had a copy on my mobile. Should I contact the police? Without Walter's approval?

Suddenly it became obvious to me. Jill would know exactly what to do.

15

Next morning, after a bad night's sleep, I opened up the gallery. Jill came in a while later. I sorted out some coffee and when we had sat down together in the office, I plunged straight into my worries.

'Jill, I need your advice. It's Walter, my Grandfather….he's in trouble.'

Jill was very alert.

'He's had a heart attack and -- he's being threatened by someone. I think that's what caused it.'

'That's terrible, Sadie. He's such a lovely man. Who's threatening him?'

'I recorded a message from his answer phone - shall I play it to you?'

I found the audio file, switched the phone on to speaker, and placed it on the table between us.

Again, the bad line -- the menacing voice, ' Alright Mr Alexander, you've got ten days to transfer the cash to the account I gave you, then we'll deliver. And if the transfer doesn't happen, you're going to get a nasty surprise.'

Jill lost her colour - she just stared at the phone in a trance.

Then she stood up and rushed into the toilet, where she vomited and coughed noisily. I could see her crouching in front of the WC, she'd been unable even to close the door.

My instincts were to go to help her - but with a shock, it came to me that Jill meeting my Grandfather, these threats and the heart attack, could be linked. Jill knew that and was thrown sideways by the recorded message.

Still crouching over the toilet, she called out, 'Sorry Sadie. Sorry about this.'

She seemed to be almost choking on her vomit, 'This is the second bout today. I shouldn't have come in….'

I kept still, and asked myself is that true?

After cleaning herself up, Jill came into the office again. She was very pale.

'I'm sorry about that - just hearing that awful phone call set me off again. It's this bug. I wish I was in a better state to do something to help.'

I kept very still, just looked straight into Jill's eyes, willed her to explain.

'What's wrong Sadie? You're….upset by all this. Who wouldn't be?'

She walked away from the table, 'I won't get too close. I'm probably stinking anyway. Why are you looking like that?'

I just kept very still. She was reading my body language. 'You can't think that I'm connected with that -- oh, Sadie.'

I was not going to take her rebuke, 'I don't know. What was the delivery about? That message was about delivering something. What was it?'

'Well -- it could be anything. What sort of things does he have delivered?'

I snapped at her, 'You know that -- paintings'. We stared at each other until she eventually looked down.

'Jill, I'm going to the police. I've no choice. This is going to kill him.'

Jill gaped at me, then took control of herself and focussed her persuasive skills on me.

'Sadie, is that a good idea? It might mean nothing

and you might disturb Walter even more. Why not give it another night to see what happens? Walter's staying in hospital overnight isn't he? I mean apart from anything else surely you've got to get his permission before you do anything ...'

I tried to think. I liked this woman but suddenly I found myself thinking -- do I trust you?

'No, I've decided. I'm going to the police and I'll take the phone as evidence.'

Jill became very thoughtful then walked round the table to sit opposite me, the phone between us.

'Alright. I'll tell you everything I know -- provided you don't go to the police.'

I kept very still. She was admitting involvement, despite her earlier words. This changed things. I made myself stay very cool.

'Jill, I'm not making any promises. Now tell me everything.'

She pleaded, 'Sadie, please. You mustn't go to the police...'

Enough. I stood up and shouted right into her face, 'Tell me what you know.'

'Right, alright. Calm down. I will. But look, I don't want this to change things between us, you know ... how we get on. I mean -- you must know how much I value you here.'

'Jill -- for heaven's sake just tell me everything you know -- everything.'

'Alright. Obviously you know that Walter was keen, extremely keen on getting hold of a Bacon self-portrait, and I've got contacts in -- the wider art market. I asked someone to ring him and try to sort something out. And that's it. I never get involved personally.'

'So you rang someone and they set up a deal with my Grandfather? To sell him a painting? How did they get hold of the painting? On the open market? Bacon paintings are a fantastic price -- so this is not the open market.'

'I said the wider art market'.

'Oh come on! Stop playing with words. You mean stolen paintings, don't you....'

'No, well not necessarily. There are some excellent digital copies as well.'

'But Walter doesn't want one of those.'

She hesitated. She was scrambling for something to convince me.

'As I said I'm not involved in the details. I just set up a connection. What happens after that is entirely between Walter and the other person.'

'Julius?'

'No, one of his contacts.'

'You mean my Grandfather is receiving stolen goods. Or rather he's trying to buy a painting that he knows is stolen.'

'Look Sadie, Walter's a good man. We both know that. I'm just telling you what I know.'

'So who is this contact of Julius? When I go to the police, that's what they'll want to know -- and if I can't tell them the name, they'll question Julius and you.'

'But I had nothing to do with that threat...'

'Then you've got nothing to fear, have you.'

She looked stunned but I was not letting her off the hook.

'And -- if I don't go to the police, this threat against my Grandfather will -- I don't know -- something awful will happen, on top of the heart attack. He won't survive. Jill, I'm not going to let him get killed.'

As I got more determined, I could see Jill was beginning to panic.

'Yes -- yes – you're right. Look, I'll tell you what I'm going to do. Julius will sort things out. He's closer to these people than I am. I don't even know them but they're rough. You can tell that from the recording. There are worlds, underworlds if you like, that Julius knows about, from his past.'

'It wasn't *him* on the phone was it?'

'That's not my father. He's definitely not into that sort of thing -- and anyway that wasn't his voice. I've never heard that voice before. Look, I've got to see my father as soon as possible. Walter's in hospital for another night, isn't he? So he'll be absolutely safe. Please don't go to the police yet, Sadie. Just give me a few hours to sort this out.'

'Jill. A few minutes ago you said you weren't connected with this. Now you're saying you'll sort it out.....'

'I know. I know -- I didn't want to lie Sadie. I hate lying, especially to you. Look, are you in this evening. Can I get in contact with you? I'll ring you as soon as I know anything. Is that alright? Please -- Walter's safety is the main thing.'

'I definitely agree with that.'

I was torn. I wanted to believe that Julius, Jill's father, could sort it out, but the greatest imperative was that my Grandfather was safe.

This was one of those points in my life where I could have avoided the oceans of trouble that followed. But I wanted to believe in Jill, so I wavered.

'Alright. I won't do anything till you contact me. And you're going to contact me this evening. Is that definite?'

She got up and started collecting her bag and phone.

'Yes, this evening. You've got to trust me Sadie. I know this is difficult but I won't let you down. Or Walter. I promise.'

Then she rushed away, leaving me in the office.

I sat facing my phone and the empty chair. It's so easy to be wise in retrospect. At that point, I was bewildered. The threatening phone call to Walter, then the discovery that Jill and her father were somehow linked, was frightening. And maybe Sean was involved, even Kyle. That voice on the phone -- and Kyle the actor. I could hardly imagine Kyle getting into that sort of thing; for a start he's Mel's brother. But I'd already had one huge surprise about him.

I tried to force myself to stay cool. I decided to lock up early and walk home to the flat. Before setting off, I switched on some of my favourite tracks to fill my head with something positive but the music did nothing for me. I switched it off and just that action took my fingers close to the that awful message on my phone and made me anxious, like having a devil locked in with my music and my favourite pictures.

I was in a state of great anxiety and indecision. I chose a different route from normal which I knew would pass a police station.

I really needed to confide in Mel, my closest friend and so cool-headed. But with the questions about Kyle and Sean hovering, I couldn't talk to her. True, I didn't have to mention Kyle to Mel, but then if she was to talk to him, all sorts of complications might emerge.

My head was in a muddle. I wanted to take some action but didn't know what, except wait to see what

Jill would come up with. But what would happen then?

I started getting near the police station. If I went in, might I incriminate my Grandfather for planning to receive stolen goods? I glanced in the doorway then walked straight past.

16

I'd forgotten that Kyle was around. He was cooking, which meant ready-made in the microwave. He was in the kitchen.

Mel saw that I was not my normal self, 'What's up babes? You ill?'

'It's Walter. He's had another heart attack. He's in hospital..'

'Oh -- you poor dear. How bad?'

'I think he'll be alright but this seems to happen every year now. I don't know how long he'll last...'

She put her arms around me and this gave me strength. I was thinking -- Mel, you don't know the half. She was far too tactful to mention again my possible inheritance, but I knew she'd be thinking of it at some point. Would I get the flat? Would she marry Justin? What then?

But my mind was focussed on the phone call I was expecting, sometime that evening.

I lied to Mel. 'I have to go round to the hospital later to see the doctor. They're going to ring me.'

'Do you want me to come with you?'

'I'll be fine. You stay in with Kyle.'

Kyle shouted us through for the meal, which was not bad by his standards. We told him about Walter's illness. Then Kyle quizzed me about my Africa trip. He avoided saying it was all a stupid waste of time but I knew he thought that. I mentioned the pause in funds, which made him sit up. I wondered how much he knew from Sean. These silly guessing games made me more angry with him. He knew I was annoyed with him -- and tiptoed around me, so nice, so infuriating.

At last my mobile rang. It was Jill. I went to the other room.

'Sadie, can we come round and see you?'

'We?' I was not meeting Julius -- I'd rather go straight to the police.

'Tariq and I. You're OK with Tariq aren't you?'

I was fine with Tariq -- but wasn't he ill? And the two of them together might be too much. They'd have some plan for dealing with me.

'Bring him along if you want to -- but not here.' I wanted to be able to get away from them if things got difficult. And I couldn't involve Mel or Kyle.

'We can meet in a quiet pub somewhere. What about the Lark round the corner from the gallery? I can be there at nine.'

I told the other two I was going out. Kyle casually asked me who I was meeting. I said the hospital.

I walked to the pub. On the way I tried to harden myself against the expected charm offensive. I was resolved to agree to nothing until after a further night's sleep.

The Lark was a noisy congenial place, the local for lots of young professionals. I eased my way through the drinkers and spied two pairs of eyes looking for me in a nook at the darker rear of the pub. They were waiting for me. They tried to sit me between them on a bench seat, close and cosy. I ignored their welcoming arms and sat opposite them. Tariq, red-eyed but apparently in control of himself, went off to get me a drink.

'Is Tariq OK?'

'A lot better, thank God. Sadie, is it alright for

Tariq to hear the message? You brought your phone didn't you?'

'Yes -- that's alright. I backed it up before I left the house, just in case I lose the phone or anything.' I thought she needed to know that, just in case....

'Good idea. Take no risks.'

Tariq returned with my coke. Normally it would be quite a treat being out with these two, but now it was an ordeal.

I looked at Tariq, 'I'll play you the message if you like....'

By this stage I could recite it by heart, even imitate the tone -- 'Alright Mr Alexander, you've got ten days.....'

Tariq listened and twisted his face in disgust, 'That's awful. Who the hell is it anyway?'

'You've never heard that voice before?'

'Never! I don't recognise it. Not at all.'

After our joint handling of drunk Baz, then seeing him stressed with Sean, I trusted him.

So I turned to Jill. 'What did Julius have to say?'

Jill nodded. We both knew this was a critical question.

'He was horrified, of course and -- he's working to get to the bottom of it. He knows the connection I mentioned -- Jim. He knows that some of his team, Jim's team that is, are pretty rough. And he's told Jim that the pressure on your Grandfather has to stop.'

'Has to stop? I see. And how has this Jim responded? And who is this Jim? Do you know him?'

'Julius is certain that the pressure will work. He's got a handle on this guy; he pushes lots of work his way so there's leverage. And he's using it.'

'Do you know this Jim guy?'

'Not really, no…'

I sat back, stared into my drink. That was something, but not much, not enough.

'So that means if nothing happens, Julius's pressure on this Jim, who you don't know, has worked. But if Walter gets some nasty surprise, it hasn't worked. Look, I'm not taking any risks with my Grandfather. He hasn't got many years left anyway but all this extra pressure is dangerous. I can't let it happen.'

Tariq spoke up, it seemed to me with real sincerity.

'Sadie, I've never pretended to like Julius, but I do respect his skills. If he says he's making Jim stop, that's it. Jim will stop. Things are black-and-white for Julius. And he can turn the screws as much as necessary.'

Jill said, 'Julius likes you Sadie and he's going to make damn sure that you're in no way hurt or upset -- and that means Walter's going to be fine.'

They were turning up the pressure, but I was unconvinced. And I didn't trust Julius. I hardened myself.

'I've met Julius. He was very rude and then later, at your prompting Jill, he tried to persuade me that he's this lovely guy. I ended up feeling -- well I know he's your father but I don't know where I am with him. Leaving Walter in his hands scares me.'

Tariq looked surprised by my little outburst -- and I thought he was about to agree with me -- then he looked down. There was a long silence. At this point I thought I'm going to have to get out of here and probably out of the gallery job.

I stood up. 'I'm sorry. I'm going now. There's nothing more to say.'

Tariq rose, came round the table and almost obstructed my departure, but not quite.

'Look Sadie, there's other things we've got to tell you. Please give us another five minutes -- and then if you have to go -- to the police or whatever, and least you'll know the consequences.'

'Meaning what?'

'Can we explain? Please...'

We both resumed our places. Me opposite them, sceptical but prepared to let them try once more.

Jill opened her hands towards me and started talking passionately, 'Sadie, we didn't want to -- burden you with this -- but if the police get involved, that will be the end of the ARW project. I won't be able to continue funding the education of the girls. They're in a terrible situation. Saving these girls from what amounts to slavery, before they've even grown-up, that's my passion. You know that.'

She started welling up. 'Seeing girls of sixteen with two or three children and more to come, their lives spent in poverty trying to feed those that survive -- I can't stand it. I can't see this happen and do nothing. If you go to the police, I'd have to cut my links with the charity.'

'But why? The money you give is from your inheritance, bonds and stuff you said...'

I looked at them both. Their downcast eyes told me that I had been very naive. I ought to have realised that as soon as I heard the telephone message to Walter.

They sat in silence. Jill had her eyes tight shut, with tears running down her face. Tariq just looked down, I guess in shame. Eventually Tariq spoke for both of them.

'This is difficult. The truth is that if you go to the police, our lives will be ruined. You might say we deserve it, but Harry doesn't. Some people think that shuffling around a few overpriced paintings is nothing. But the fact is we've broken the law and so would have to face the consequences. Jill and I set that against what is happening with these girls in Africa. Their lives have been freed and there are dozens more waiting and hoping. We can't let them down.'

He was right. I knew that in my heart. Setting the one against the other, the gross imbalance was so clear -- a small crime in a crazy investors' art market -- against a massive good.

'But you're breaking the law. I know that you two want to help these young women -- and I really want to help them myself, but....'

Jill opened her eyes in gratitude. She was sobbing. 'Oh thank you. Thank you Sadie. It's such a relief to hear you say that.'

I was near tears myself, but I had to make Walter safe. 'What you're saying is that the funds for the African girls comes from art thefts.'

Silence. Then Jill said, 'Some of the funds, only some...'

'From art thefts. That's the truth, isn't it?'

'Alright, yes. That's the truth.'

'And the people doing these thefts are you two, Julius. And I guess that Sean is involved. Anyone else?'

'Not really. Sean's friend, Kyle, sometimes helps out, but he's not that much involved. Basically it's the four of us. Obviously the fewer involved, the safer...'

What did she mean by *friend*? Anyway I was not
going to admit to knowing Kyle.

'Alright -- so who's Jim?'

Silence -- then Tariq stepped in, 'That's what
Julius's finding out. We think it's either Sean or Kyle.
He's talking to them both.'

He wasn't talking to Kyle. Kyle was with Mel at the
flat, but they didn't know that.

'So Jim is a fiction...it's really Sean's voice in that
phone message.'

Another pause then, 'Or Kyle's. We don't know
yet. Jim was -- the code name we used for the
person who made the threat.'

I was reaching my limit, 'Code name? What do
you take me for? Look -- you've got to get Walter out
of danger. For ever. Otherwise I'm going to the police.
Completely out of danger in a way that I can totally
believe.'

Tariq said, 'We can do this, Sadie. Honestly, we
can. Julius will sort it out. He'll stop these threats.'

'Will? You said earlier he'd done it ...'

Jill said, 'Alright, it's work in progress. But he'll do
it. He will. I'll make him. I promise you, Sadie. He'll
finish the job.' I was unconvinced.

'And what about the financial deal? The money
my Grandfather still owes?'

Jill said, 'That's all scrapped -- or frozen rather. As
far as I know. No, sorry, I do know Walter has paid a
deposit on the Bacon painting and has been loaned
something, another painting -- as a sort of security.
That's what normally happens. And then when the
Bacon is available, ready for delivery, the rest of the
cash is handed over.'

'When the Bacon is available. So it's not stolen
yet?'

'I'm sure we have the painting now. We definitely have the painting. But the theft has not been discovered. Or at least it hasn't hit the press yet.'

'So what's the problem?'

'I'm sorry to have to tell you this, but Walter's in difficulties, I mean financial difficulties. Currently he's not able to pay...'

'And that's why he was threatened...'

Jill hesitated. 'I'm afraid so. I'm really sorry. But now we're going to freeze the current situation. Isn't that right, Tariq?'

'Yes, that must be right, whatever gives Sadie and Walter peace. That's where we are now. Look Sadie, you've got to give Julius another twenty four hours to nail the thing down'.

I looked him full in the eyes, 'Tariq, I haven't got to do anything.'

He paused, 'Sorry. That was a stupid thing to say. What I mean is we need twenty four hours, for the sake of those girls.'

I was sick of all this. 'Tariq, Walter will be out of hospital in twenty four hours, back in his flat!'

'Ok -- what about by midday tomorrow? Please Sadie...'

Jill had her eyes closed tight. They were both pleading with me. I had to give them a few hours, didn't I? I couldn't go into a police station, report them, wreck their lives, remove Harry from his parents, and probably impose more pressures on Walter, if he was planning to receive stolen property. I had no choice.

'When I say not a minute after midday tomorrow, I mean it. You know where to find me.'

Jill opened her eyes, 'In the gallery?'

'Yes, in the gallery.'

She took my hands and whispered, 'Thank you so much Sadie...'

She clasped my hands tightly. I'm ashamed to admit that I welcomed this. It was about trust, perhaps affection, affection after bruising events. Her spell was weaker. I knew I must hold myself further away from Jill.

I quickly withdrew my hands and stood up for a second time.

'I'm going now. I need to think through how I'm going to approach this with my Grandfather. Tomorrow afternoon, when he comes out. Depending on what I hear from you.'

Tariq also stood up and came round the table, 'Of course. One more thing, can you promise that no one learns about any of this. If the way that we fund the African project, was even hinted to another person, even your Grandfather or your closest friends or your boyfriend ...'

'What boyfriend?'

'OK, sorry -- I thought you lived with....

'Mel, my flat-mate?'

'Right -- well Mel then. But the point I'm making is that every deal means risk. Apart from anything else there are loads of journalists out there who would give a lot to know where these missing artworks are. You're involved in our secrets now Sadie..'

He saw my grimace at that and tried to backtrack, 'What I mean is that we trust you with our secrets and if the slightest hint gets out, the consequences are going to be horrific.'

'You mean I'd get into trouble with the police?'

Jill stepped in and spoke over Tariq. 'You know nothing. Right? We're the ones who'd get into trouble with police and the law, but it's the African girls who'd be the losers....'

I nodded agreement. Then Tariq hugged me. That hug and Jill holding my hands, meant something, but I had to keep them at a distance. I didn't respond.

I felt stunned by all of these events. I made my way home, like a robot, not able to think.

Kyle was still there with Mel. They had said Kyle, Sean's friend, was just a casual help but I didn't know what to believe. I pretended I'd been on a hospital visit and added some plausible detail about Walter's condition. Then I escaped to my bedroom for an early night, and tried to think out my options again.

I couldn't go to the police. It would wreck the charity and it could incriminate Walter. That was impossible. So the obvious move was for me to get the hell out of Gallery Elite and cut off contact with Jill and the rest of them. I'd just resign and avoid further contact.

So what next? One idea was to see if my friend in Brussels knew about any jobs, but then I couldn't leave Walter, especially while there was any risk of a further heart attack. So I'd have to pick up something locally. So with that decided, I tried to sleep.

17

Next morning, I was dithering again. The idea of resigning was still there, but held in reserve. I didn't have to open the gallery as Jill was already in the office. She got up as I entered. We were both serious; the over-friendly greetings were in the past. Our old boss-temp relationship was over. We sat down at the table opposite each other, the same as the previous day. She plunged into her explanation.

'Julius has sorted it. It's over. It was almost certainly Sean, though Kyle's the actor. Julius couldn't get out of Sean exactly who made the two phone calls, but Sean set the thing up. He admitted it. He hadn't realised it was your Grandfather. He's very sorry, believe it or not. He's been threatening clients who don't pay up on the dot, without our knowledge.'

I didn't think Kyle would do a thing like that, but if it was an actor-type challenge, perhaps he would. After all he didn't know it was my Grandfather -- and Jill didn't know I lived with Kyle's sister. I planned to keep that quiet.

I suddenly thought of me passing Sean the key for the filing cabinet and him asking me to not tell Jill. Another time, I'd found the filing cabinet unlocked when I had definitely locked it. I had assumed Jill had been in after I'd left, but perhaps Sean paid another visit... Then there was the news article Julius got so upset about.

'Did they do that kneecapping?'

'Oh that -- no that wasn't anything to do with us. Julius thought it was at first.'

'And what about Walter's payments. Or non

payments?'

'The finances are frozen till Walter gets the cash. Or if he wants to return the painting we loaned him, that's fine. Whatever he wants....'

'And what about the Bacon painting? Suppose it takes him years to get the funds? Or decides to not take it at all?'

'We'll just leave it stored away. Wait till another Bacon enthusiast appears.'

She'd said -- the painting we loaned him. I should have asked about that. What painting and where was it?

Anyway I was at another decision point.

'Jill, I've got to say I'm only eighty per cent convinced. It's not exactly proof, is it...'

Jill became quite intense at this stage, 'Sadie, I promise promise promise that no harm will come to Walter. You can personally march me into a police station if this proves wrong....'

'It would be too late then, wouldn't it, Jill. Walter would probably be dead.'

'Please don't say that Sadie. Walter's in no risk. You're in no risk. What can I say to get you over the last twenty per cent? And if you want to get even more involved in the African project, that would be great.'

I stared at her. I was being bribed. She was floundering around looking for ways to get me on board, as she would put it. And I wanted to be on board, even though I knew it meant pretending crimes weren't being committed. But for a noble cause!

I didn't take my situation seriously enough. I watched her trying to hook me. And I wanted to be hooked, to please her. Looking back, I feel ashamed.

'Now that I know how you fund it, I can't get more involved. I mean I'd love to, but...'

She sat up and looked me straight in the eyes.

'Sadie, you don't know anything. You're an innocent bystander, an outsider really. We haven't had this conversation either now or last night. And in any case, Africa ARW has other sources of funding apart from us. You've been to Africa. You've seen the problems.'

'I know, but I'd still be hiding evidence from the police.'

'How? If you don't know anything? And if the thing ever falls apart, you're out of the loop. But it's not going to fall apart, and we're going to close it down anyway, in a year or two.'

'Are you?'

'Probably. You've seen how difficult Sean is, but we still need his skills to finish off some deals. That's something else you don't know. Right?'

'I suppose so. Yes, right.'

'You know nothing about our secrets -- and Walter will be safe. Is that agreed?'

I took a deep breath, then found myself saying, 'Alright....agreed.'

'Good. I knew we could sort this between us.'

She came round and gave me a hug. I let her.

Mission accomplished, she said, 'Can I leave you now? Do you mind?'

'Walter comes out this afternoon. I have to be there...'

'Of course you do. I should have remembered. If I'm back by one, will that be alright?'

On the way out, she gave me another quick hug. God, she knew how to handle me.

I had decided to stay overnight with Walter till I was sure he could cope by himself. I still had my own bedroom from when I lived there when my father and brother went off to New Zealand. Alice was doing some extra hours so someone was going to be around most of the time. I took the afternoon off to welcome him back home. Alice had been around earlier to shop and prepare some food. As I petted the cat, I tried to think out a way of letting Walter know that the threats were lifted. But I had to approach the matter gently and gauge how he reacted. I couldn't risk him having another heart attack. I had to do something because he would find that the telephone message was deleted.

Walter's arrival and settling in went fine. He was able to mount the steps to the house entrance, slowly but without help from the paramedic. He still looked very tired, in contrast to the cat who was exultantly happy and would not leave him alone.

'Well one creature in this world certainly loves me.'

'Two creatures Grandfather. I'm getting jealous.'

'My darling, you're not a creature. You don't know how grateful I am to you. I've never been much good at talking about feelings. That's what your grandmother said, but this time you've pulled me through. And Sadie, there aren't going to be many more times. You know that, don't you?'

'Grandfather -- please! I'm not going to lose you any time soon. Right?'

We had a good evening. Alice had left food to be heated up and some salad, then later we watched a DVD of Walter's favourite Mozart opera, during which he fell asleep. Later I brought him a hot drink as he lay in bed.

'You know Sadie, I didn't think I was coming home this time.'

'Well you are home Grandfather -- and in rather good shape...'

'True. It reminds me that I must show you where I've left all the details of financial and other things, so that you'll know what to do when I don't come back.'

'Right, but I'm in no hurry for that, thank you very much.'

I kissed him good night.

On the following morning, he seemed to be perking up, so after breakfast I braced myself to enter the danger zone.

'Grandfather, there's some other stuff I want to talk to you about, some stuff Jill mentioned...'

Walter looked at me warily, 'Your boss. What did *she* have to say?'

'She was chatting about her main business, I mean getting hold of paintings for clients ...'

'Oh that, yes. She told me all about that when you brought her over. In fact she tried to talk me into buying something but -- well -- that's all more or less in the past.'

So he was in denial. But I had to proceed, 'When I told her about your illness, she was very sorry. She asked me to pass on a message to you. She said -- don't worry about anything. She'll handle it. I didn't really understand what she meant, but she seemed to think it was important.'

He looked at me sharply, 'I see. Did she say anything else?'

'Not really. She was a bit vague. Were you going to buy something from her? I think she was saying there's no hurry about anything.'

'No hurry. About what exactly?'

'I don't know. I mean I don't know how far things have got between the two of you, but she was saying everything's in control. There's nothing to worry about.'

Walter looked bewildered. He was silent and closed his eyes. I'd gone too far but I couldn't stop myself. He was going to discover the deleted phone message anyway.

'She said something about threats. I didn't understand that, but it was nothing to do with her and she really regretted it all. The threats are going to stop now, have stopped she said. So there's nothing more to worry about, is there, Grandfather?'

Walter put his head back on the chair, still with his eyes closed.

'Are you alright, Grandfather? Do you need anything?'

'I'm alright, my dear. Just trying to work out what that means.'

'She means the deal is frozen. No more threats. And if the funds don't become available, that'll be fine as well. No more problems.'

Suddenly he opened his eyes wide and looked closely into mine, 'You know, don't you? You're trying to protect me ...'

'Everything's sorted out now. Jill and her father are sorting things out. They're very sad that you were put under pressure.'

'Her father! I don't trust that man...'

'I know, but Jill's different. We can trust Jill.'

'Can we? I don't know what to say, darling. I feel so ashamed to have got into all of this. And then with losing all that money. I made some stupid investments. Everything's changed. I lost a lot. And it was meant for you ...'

He looked at me with tearful eyes and a mournful face. I put my arms around his neck and kissed him. At least he was still alive.

'I know that Grandfather, but it's alright now...'

He recovered quite quickly. We both avoided further discussion of the painful subjects, including the deleted phone message which he must have seen was gone.

Next morning, I called in on my way to work. He was almost his normal self. Perhaps overnight he had come to believe that the threat really was lifted. I stayed to see Alice and had coffee with Walter, then went to the gallery for morning opening.

18

I had to talk to Kyle without Mel being around or even knowing we'd met. I wanted to know what his involvement was with the thefts – and let him know that the two of us were finished, if we were ever really started. Also I wanted to know if he knew about my close encounter with Sean. I felt furious with Kyle at the thought of all this and whatever he'd been up to with Sean. I wanted to put him on the spot. Next evening, I marched into the Park Tavern where he worked as a barman and told him bluntly that I wanted to talk with him.

'But I'm working tonight, Sadie. You can see...'

'Kyle, you're not working on your own and the place is quiet. You can take a short break.'

'OK, OK. Go and sit over there and I'll join you.'

Kyle's pub was a pseudo traditional tacky sort of place. The wooden tables felt sticky. On the wall were prints of hunting scenes and early racing cars, a cheap job lot. There was nowhere to sit for privacy so I just got as far as possible from the bar and the few other punters. It seemed a depressing place to work.

Kyle poured a white wine for me and a beer for himself, fixed things up with his fellow barman and came over.

'There you go. It's on me this time.'

'Right.'

'That's been your favourite as long as I've known you.'

He was being nice but I had to go for it. 'Kyle, I

want you to tell me about Sean. I didn't know that you lived with him.'

He looked fairly sheepish then said, 'I was completely gobsmacked at seeing you. I really was. I mean I knew you worked for Jill and you'd met Sean but ...it was a real shock.'

'So it was a shock for both of us. That's why I want to sort things out. I mean, how close are you to Sean?'

He looked at me sharply. 'I was going to ask you the same question...'

I was outraged. How dare he! 'Look, personally I never want to see Sean again, ever. We're colleagues, that's all. I just came round about the gallery web site. Now what about you?'

He became silent and looked as if he wasn't going to give me an answer.

'I don't know what to say. That's a private thing you're asking..'

'Of course it's private. Look, you and I always got on OK and well, Mel's always trying to shove us together -- and then suddenly to find you're living with somebody else, maybe as partners. That was a surprise. And then to find that it's a bloke. That was unbelievable.'

'Well don't believe it. It's all in the past anyway.'

'What's in the past? So you were with Sean?'

He thought for a while before saying, 'Isn't everyone a bit bi? It wasn't a proper relationship. I mean it wasn't romantic or anything -- and now, it's more or less over. Sean's deep. Alright I admit I had a thing about him, but as far as he's concerned, I'm past my sell-by date.'

Was he saying he was a younger guy who had been used? A nice arrangement!

He lifted his head and looked at me closely and almost whispered, 'Please don't dump me or anything, Sadie. That would be hard to bear, on top of everything else.'

I was taken by surprise. He was pleading with me. Nothing so serious had ever happened between us but he obviously believed we were in some sort of relationship. I felt my anger softening.

'I'm not going to dump anybody, Kyle, but this changes things. Know what I mean?'

'I know I'm not the person you thought I was – a 100% straight, out-of-work actor with a simple life.'

We half smiled at each other. At least there was no hint of Sean telling him about my mistake.

I wanted to press him about the work he did with Sean. I couldn't reveal what I had learned from Jill.

'You work with Sean as well, don't you? What do you do exactly?'

' Nothing much. Sometimes he and Julius need an extra pair of hands to lug paintings and things around. I mean I'm a trained actor and acting's the work I'm after, me and a thousand others – and I do a bit of that for Sean on the side. Then there's the job here which pays almost nothing. I don't earn much; that's why I come to scrounge food from you and Mel.'

'So what paintings are you moving around?'

'Heaven knows. I just turn up, lift and carry and put down again. They're always in wraps anyway. They've got a small lockup at the back of your gallery.'

'The back of Gallery Elite? Where?'

'Next to your front door, there's an alleyway -- right? Just down there. It's just a storeroom. I thought you'd know more about it than me, working with Jill in the office.'

There was a call from the bar, 'How you doing Kyle? I need some help here.'

He rolled his eyes. 'I'll have to go….'

'What do you mean – you do a bit of acting for Sean on the side?'

'It's a bit of a laugh. He's into security systems, so I play the art freak to distract the guards while he noses around and takes snaps of their setup. I know it doesn't sound too good, but -- well….'

From the bar, a stronger call, 'Kyle, we've got customers….'

'So what does Sean want this information for?'

'I better be off. Heaven knows. He never tells me anything. You stay put and finish your drink.'

'Hang on Kyle. Does Sean ever get you to make phone calls, when people haven't paid up?'

'No, nothing like that. I'll see you at Mel's in a day or two.'

And off he went behind the bar. I watched him as I finished my drink. He said he was some sort of dumb labourer with a bit of play acting for a laugh. But surely he must have realised that Sean's interest in security systems was not innocent. Alright he's an actor, but he couldn't have been involved in the threats to Walter, could he?

And he'd said the relationship with Sean, whatever it had been, was over. I'd arrived at the pub angry with Kyle – and left saying he thinks we're in some sort of low level relationship, so I suppose we might be. The 'please don't dump me' had surprised me. I had a slight rush of affection for him, and pity that he was involved in this mess.

I finished my wine and as I left the pub, waved to Kyle. He blew me a kiss.

19

Next morning, I arrived to find the gallery open. As I walked between the two rows of paintings towards my desk, I could hear a row going on in the office. It was Jill and Marion. They went on and on. Marion's pedantic rumbling alternating with Jill becoming shrill. Jill had told me there was a meeting about publicity for ARW. They hadn't invited me. I'd seen the web site and it was weak. Screeds of text, a few small photographs and no consistent colour theme. They seemed to be locked in a stalemate, so I decided to try to help.

I knocked on the door of the office then marched in to face two pairs of glaring eyes, 'Can I make you both a coffee?'

They both gaped at me as if I was from another world, then Jill came to, recalled that she needed to be nice to me – and perhaps that she had invited me to be more involved in ARW.

'That sounds like a brilliant idea, and we ought to seek Sadie's opinion? We're getting nowhere. We have to resolve this thing Marion, so let's see what Sadie's got to say.'

Marion hesitated, then said rather fiercely, 'Jill, with all due respect to Sadie, these decisions have to be made by you and I.'

'Of course, but it might help us move forward to hear what someone else says.'

'Well as long as you understand where decisions are to be rightly made. I suppose we'd better start with my website since you're making such a fuss about it.'

Her website, that explains a lot.

I said, 'Let's have coffee first -- and a chocolate biscuit.'

Marion immediately softened. I had learned about that weakness waiting in airports on the trip to Africa.

Jill saw an opportunity. 'Yes, I've actually got your favourites, Marion...'

'Which? Oh those. I've gone off those now. But I won't refuse.'

Then we spent a few minutes sipping and chewing and comparing our different preferences in biscuits. Marion had a wide knowledge, almost an expertise. In thinking about this and about her ARW web site, the phrase obsessive-compulsive popped into my mind.

I could see a challenge ahead. Marion had edited the website. It was her baby and it was boring. I could do so much better. But that meant getting more involved in ARW, which I'd said to Jill I couldn't. But I really wanted to.

They sat me down in front of Jill's laptop and the front page of the ARW site.

Jill said, 'Now tell us what you think...you don't mind if she's blunt, do you Marion?'

'Of course not. I respect honesty...and I've no doubt that some changes could be made.'

I gently made the obvious points, 'Larger and more photos would be great. We took lots last week.'

'You did Sadie. Remember, I haven't seen them yet. Anything else?'

'Most people pay online now, not by cheque. There are a number of options we could organise. And what about looking at some other charity sites. See how the competition operates?'

Marion said, more to Jill, 'Those are quite useful

comments Sadie is making, but my problem is time.'

'I know how hard you work Marion. And this is an extra burden for which you were never trained....'

'Quite! I never thought that it was necessary, but of course I'm always ready to learn. Have you any other comments, Sadie?'

'Well I think of colour, and consistency from page to page.'

'We don't want any flashy gimmicks, thank you very much.'

'True. But a quiet colour theme, consistent with the schools and the area, could hold the site together.'

'Umm -- possibly. But I'm really not sure about doing that sort of thing. Anything else?'

'When I look at any web site, I always think of the phrase 'sense of audience'. Do you follow me?'

Marion said, 'That's a rather abstract idea, Sadie. You'd better explain....'

And a few minutes later, I had her, Marion that is. It was much easier than I expected. To her credit, rather than becoming upset at having the limitations of the site revealed, she appeared to understand and accept my points, discreetly cheered on by Jill. Perhaps she really wanted to get out of working on the site. Quite suddenly it was agreed that I was taking over.

Jill was delighted. I was delighted. Apart from all else, it was a constructive way of using the empty hours in the gallery. Marion launched herself into a fuss about editorial control but we worked out how to proceed. I would draft out a new site then we would meet to discuss and refine.

Later I realised I'd given in to temptation. I had

said I would not get more involved in ARW because Jill had used it as a bribe, to keep me away from the police. But then I thought, Walter is safe, I'm safe – and it's going to be fun to sort out this web site – and much easier now that I had visited the schools and got to know the pupils a little.

20

When I got back to the flat that evening, Kyle was putting together a meal. Mel and I laid the kitchen table while Kyle operated the microwave. Mel had been to visit my Grandfather. Her parents and grandparents lived in Manchester so she had adopted Walter as a sort of family.

I asked Mel how she thought Walter looked a week after the heart attack.

'Not well. To be honest I saw a big change -- and Sadie, I made a bit of a hash of my visit. I might have upset him.'

'Why? What happened?'

'It was a bit weird. I can't make sense of it. We'd been chatting away then he went off to the loo. He was away for an age and I was getting worried. I was really just pottering around in his living room then I noticed something about the big painting he has over the fireplace, that big cubist face.'

'That old thing. It's been there as long as I remember.'

'Well it seemed to have got raised off the wall a bit, just two or three mills, on some sort of ridge behind.'

'Really. I've never noticed that'.

'I thought it was just some fancy fitting, then I found a tiny lever underneath, moved it and the painting swung open – nearly knocked me over actually. There was a recess behind, with another painting in it. I was shocked.'

I thought – oh God, given the threat and Jill's

revelations. What now?

'Sadie – are you OK?'

'Sorry. I was just thinking – why've I never noticed that? Two paintings in one, sounds clever. Come to think of it, he must have showed it to me a while back. Anyway, what's the hidden painting?'

'A Francis Bacon. One of his nasty heads. It was quite a shock.'

I was speechless. Have they delivered the painting after all. And what should I say to Mel?

I struggled. 'Not a real Bacon?'

'I don't think so, more of a print or a photo or something. Hasn't he ever shown you it?'

Then I saw that Kyle had gone very still. Mel had her back to him but to me, the impact of her words on him was obvious. And I was reeling.

'Sadie -- Sadie, what's up? Hasn't he ever shown you it?'

'No, never. When he showed me the second painting holder, long ago, there must have been something different, not a Bacon.'

I felt intense irritation at Walter for not telling me about the recess, at myself for never noticing it – and at Mel for finding it.

'No, it's coming back to me. I'd just forgotten…'

'It's not like you to forget a thing like that….'

'I know, I know. I think there was a different painting there when I saw it. A Hockney or something.'

Lies upon lies, and Mel could read me so easily.

Kyle started moving about again. He half turned. We avoided looking at each other.

Mel looked at me. 'Sadie, are you alright? You're upset, aren't you?'

'Not really. I'm just shocked. What happened when he came back?'

'Oh, I can hardly bear to tell you now. Here, give me your hand.'

'What? What happened? Tell me.'

'When Walter had sat down, I asked him about it, of course, and then things went really odd. He played dumb. He said it's nothing, nothing of importance. So I said it was a cute idea and just opened it up, said things like -- we ought to market this idea, stupid stuff like that. I knew I'd done the wrong thing because he began to look ill. Sadie, I was frightened that I'd done real harm, but how was I to know? He was panting and could hardly speak.'

'Oh God – is he alright?'

'He's fine now. Honestly. I mean at the time I got really scared. I didn't know what to do, ring 999 or you or what. Then he became normal again more or less. Then he said I had to get him a glass of water and some particular pills and then go…..he was quite brusque.'

'So you left him?'

'No, of course not. I got him the pills then made some tea and biscuits and stuff, stayed with him to check he was safe. I wasn't going to leave him till I was certain he was well and stable. He was tired. He wanted me to go but I stayed and chatted and chatted till I was certain he was fine. Then I came back here.'

I was stupidly furious with Mel for finding this recess and for making Walter unwell. And with Kyle for his involvement or whatever?

I burst out, 'And I suppose I've got to sort this mess out now?'

'No – of course not. He's alright now. What's got into you Sadie? I've just told you what happened. He's fine now. I mean how was I to know he'd get upset?'

'Sorry. I get a bit uptight at the thought of him

being ill. He's just out of hospital.'

Of course it wasn't only that. Why had I not noticed this recess that Mel had spotted so easily? Why had I not asked myself where the Bacon was to go. If Walter was going to get a genuine Bacon, surely it had to be hidden away so that the likes of Mel couldn't stumble over it. And having this discussion in the hearing of Kyle made me more wretched.

I calmed down and said to Mel, 'I didn't mean to get worked up like that. It's all got so messy. I'd better go and ring him.'

I went to my room and fished out my phone.

'Walter Alexander here...'

'Hi Grandfather....it's Sadie.'

'Oh, thanks for ringing my dear. Mel said she was on her way to you....is she there?'

'I'm by myself. She told me what happened...'

'Did she? Yes I took a dizzy turn while she was here. It was soon over. She was very helpful.'

'Yes she told me everything that happened, what she discovered...'

'Oh that....you didn't know, did you...'

'No...'

I waited for him to tell me more -- and waited.

'Sorry darling. I was shaken up when she....'

'I know.'

'She told you? Sadie, what else does she know?'

'Nothing. She knows nothing – and it will stay that way. All that matter is closed now. Right?'

'If you say so Sadie....I want to believe you -- but I'm not certain I can.'

'I'm convinced of it Grandfather. Are you alright now?'

'I think so. All the better for speaking with you…'
'Good. Don't worry. See you soon.'
'Yes my dear.'
'Bye Grandfather.'
'Goodbye darling – and thank you.'

When I went into the kitchen, Mel asked me if Walter was alright.

'He seems fine. No damage done. And Mel, thanks for visiting him. I'm sorry I was so, you know, worked up.'

'That's alright. But he's at it now.' She nodded towards Kyle. 'He's giving me the cold freeze, like he did when he was a teenager. You two haven't had a row or something have you?'

'Look Sis, I've just had a rough day. Can we just forget about it please.'

'Fine. Fine.'

'Now can you two just sit down and we'll eat.…'

Kyle was working in the pub that evening but before he left, while Mel was in her room, he turned to me very seriously.

"Sadie, I didn't know that was your Grandfather… I'm sorry, I just didn't realise.'

'What do you mean?'

'I delivered that painting, the one that Mel found and I hung it in the recess thing.'

I stared at him. 'Were you alone?'

'Sean was there. He was the one that talked to your granddad. I was just labouring.'

'What did they say?'

'Something about deposit, temporary, that sort of thing. I wasn't listening.'

'Were they friendly or angry with each other?'

'Oh, you know, it was business, nothing special.'

I got my phone and played back the threatening message to him. He was clearly shocked.

I said, 'That's your voice, isn't it...'

He looked at me in horror. 'NO -- I wouldn't do a thing like that Sadie.'

'It was you. You were just doing what Sean told you to...'

'THAT ISN'T ME. Honestly Sadie. I wouldn't lie, not to you.'

'Well who is it?'

He was silent and shrugged.

'Sean?'

'I don't know. I don't know if he can do that sort of voice.'

'So who?'

'I just don't know.'

Then Mel came back.

'Are you two having a row? I heard you shouting from my room...'

Kyle and I looked at each other. He said, 'It was a pretend fight. She was teasing me again.'

He looked me in the eyes. 'We're still friends really, aren't we?'

'Are we? Don't ask stupid questions Kyle. Aren't you late for work?'

He's lost track of time and rushed off.

21

Next day I arrived at the gallery just before eleven to find it was unlocked. The lights were on in the office so I assumed Jill was in. On the reception desk was a large garish bunch of flowers, a box of chocolates and a card with my name on it. Jill knows I avoid chocolates and that carrying huge bunches of flowers home would be a pain.

I peered into the office and saw Julius. He looked up from his newspaper and waved to me. My heart sank as I realised this was all some sort of apology from him.

He came out of the office and we faced each other over the mass of flowers. I was fairly determined to keep my distance. He seemed to sense that. I feared he might come around the desk and try to hug me -- and that was never going to happen.

'I just wanted to say to your face, Sadie, I'm really really sorry.'

I found his macho pleading style unconvincing but beneath the bald head were Jill's eyes'

'Sadie, those threats on Walter were unforgivable and I honestly wish they had never happened.'

I couldn't tell whether he believed what he was saying. I was certainly not going to let him off lightly.

'You don't even know for certain who made the threats, do you?'

He paused, then spoke thoughtfully, as to an equal, 'Sadie, we don't know much for certain in this life. We make guesses -- about people, what their motives are. Sometimes we guess well. I'm pretty certain who it was. At the moment I still need that guy's skills, sadly.'

' But why don't you replace him? Get someone else with those skills?'

'I'm working on that but they aren't thick on the ground. And to be honest, he won't go till he's ready. Tariq's picking stuff up, but now he's gone a bit weird. Believe me, I'd get out of the business completely if it wasn't for Jill. To be honest, I'd sell this place, but it's her baby. I won't tell you how much it costs to keep it open. You know her Sadie. You know how passionate she is -- she won't be budged. Saving those African girls is all she thinks about -- and I admire her for it. I don't feel these things as strongly. I wish I did -- it might be with getting older. I mean I used to feel things much more. You know that I did an art degree don't you; I was very passionate about that.'

'Jill told me about that.'

'Did she tell you where I did it?'

'Was it an OU degree?'

'Yes. But I was locked up at the time.'

Tariq had told me that already but why did Julius tell me? He was trying to get me on his side…

'In prison? What on earth were you doing there?'

'Drugs -- possession. I was stupid, got into deep water and didn't know when to stop. Anyway there aren't many people I tell that to. I tell everyone about the degree. It opened my eyes to a world I didn't even know existed -- I mean the art world. I'll tell you Sadie, it was a revelation. Colour has a big effect on me you know, it's linked with emotions. Most people don't understand that. For heaven's sake, we don't even know if we see the same things. Look at all the reds in these paintings. How do you know that you are seeing the same as I'm seeing? You don't, do you.'

'That's true. But tell me, do you like these paintings?'

'Not really, but I don't tell Jill that. I leave the choice to Jill.'

'But you do know that your son's paintings are a lot better, don't you?'

'Baz? You're not serious?'

'I certainly am.'

'I knew he played around with paints but I've never seen them. Are you saying that they ought to be up in this gallery?'

'They need to be somewhere. Some of Baz's paintings are better than some of the ones in here. He's a member of the family, so he ought to get a chance.'

'Sadie, you surprise me. You must tell that to Jill.'

'Well that won't help Baz, will it? Both of you seem to dislike the guy and won't take him seriously. I know he's not easy – and he's got a drink problem. But he's got a decent woman trying to sort him out. Have you met Eva?'

'I've seen her. Plump!'

'And that's a sin? Do you ever use a mirror?'

He glared at me, then softened. 'Alright, point taken.'

'What's important is that she's good-natured and she's on his side. Getting somewhere with the paintings might help.'

'And I've neglected him. Is that what you're saying?'

I'd needled him now. He'd left the confessional and was sliding towards anger.

'Julius, am I being too uppity again – or what?'

He was silent, chastened perhaps. 'No – that's another thing I'm sorry about. It's my background, pokes me in the ribs now and then.'

'And then you poke other people…'

'My, you're a sharp one when your hackles are raised.' He spread out his hands in that all-embracing way. 'And don't I just deserve it? But look Sadie, seriously, you're an enormous help to Jill – and you're good for her. You're her friend – and I want to thank you for that as well.'

I was touched but told myself to stop being stupid. I swallowed and said, 'Alright then. Let's not get too emotional.

'No. Right. I'll sort out something about Baz and his paintings. It's going to be an uphill struggle.'

'Good -- that's the right thing to do.'

We looked at each other for a few moments, then he said in a jokey voice, 'Well, I've said what I came to say so I'll go now.'

And he marched off down the gallery. He gave a funny sort of two hands wave as he reached the door. He knew I was watching him and he knew he'd pulled me around. And he was right. He was going to do something for his son – and we both shared an interest in his daughter's well-being. I can't say I liked Julius Carruthers, but under the prickly outside there was some sort of heart.

22

Two days later, I was at my usual perch at the reception desk, working on the ARW site, when I saw someone peering in through the gallery glass door. Eva's substantial figure appeared and she mouthed, *'Is she in?'*

I called out, 'Jill? No.' Then she vanished.

I walked the length of the gallery to see what was going on. Eva was getting some paintings out of a taxi and resting them against the outside wall. I joined her as she paid off the taxi.

She was flustered but triumphant, 'I've brought Baz's paintings. There's only the three…'

'But what's Jill going to say?'

'Julius rang Baz and told him he wanted his paintings up in Gallery Elite as an experiment – only the three – but that's a start, isn't it.'

We stood facing each other, with the three framed paintings beside us, on the pavement facing the wall. Nobody had spoken to me about this. I couldn't put them up in the gallery without hearing from Julius or Jill.

'Eva, does Jill know about this arrangement?'

'She must do. Julius must have spoken to her -- surely?'

We stood looking at each other. Some splatters of rain fell.

Eva seemed to realize that I was uncertain, 'We'd better get them out of the rain.'

She took hold of two. I lifted the other and handled the powerfully sprung door. We placed them on the floor against the white gallery wall, but

facing outwards this time. They included the one Baz
had shown me a while back. The three were all in a
cosmic subconscious realm, but quite distinct from
each other. This time it was more obvious to me which
way round they should go.

'Sadie, do you really like them?'

'Yes. I honestly do. I love the primary colours and
the way they edge into these darker areas – quite
powerful. If this is Baz's subconscious, his real life
must seem tame…'

'That's wonderful. I'll tell him that; he'll be thrilled.
He calls you St Sadie, because of what you've done
for him.'

Somebody else had called me that. They'd
been talking about me. I said to myself, stop being
paranoid.

I definitely did not want to thrill Baz, but what was
to be done with his paintings?

Eva read my thoughts. 'Julius said we're to
replace the far three of the red paintings with these.'

The 'only three' and the position, were too specific
not to have come from Julius or perhaps Jill, so I
swallowed hard and we set about mounting them.
This took a while to get them lined up at the right
height.

The displaced paintings went into the office.
Then I reckoned we both needed some coffee and
there was some hot in the machine. We took one
of the office seats into the gallery so that we could
sit together, sip our drinks and admire the three
paintings. I have to say they looked more than just
presentable, much more.

Eva and I sat like naughty children at the end
of some adventure, admiring the results. She was

thrilled. She had pulled off a coup for herself and for Baz.

After a few slightly giggly moments, we settled down and I decided to take advantage of our new friendship, to quiz her more.

'Why isn't Baz here, for the hanging?'

'Oh he was nervous about getting into a row with Jill.'

'I see. So tell me. How is Baz's work with Sean going? You said they were doing some business together…'

'Oh me and my big mouth. Look Sadie, I'm not supposed to say anything about that…'

After a pause, I said, 'Right – but about what?'

'I can't say. Baz told me to not tell a soul. Something they're working on, that's all.'

'Look, I know that Baz wants to be involved in the business…'

'Yes, he does.'

'And now that he has some paintings up here, in a way, he is.'

'Yes. You're right. That's probably all it is.'

'But that's not what Sean and Baz are plotting….'

'Something to do with paintings. That's all I know.'

'Look Eva, I've gone out of my way to help you – and we're friends, aren't we?'

'Oh and I really appreciate it Sadie. I'd have got nowhere without you – but I don't know what Baz is up to with Sean. And to be honest, I don't want to know. I don't trust Sean and he just ignores me completely.'

'Really. I wish I could say the same. You must hear what they're on about, surely?'

'The odd word, but it doesn't make any sense to me….'

And that was as far as I could get – and may have
been all she knew.

It was time to move on, 'Eva, I need to think about
closing the gallery now. We ought to prepare some
labels for Baz's paintings. Ask him to email me titles
and dates and something about the themes.'

We parted, both happy at this progress. I looked
again at Baz's paintings and said to myself, whatever
Jill may think, we've done the right thing.

23

Next day it was raining and my good mood was also dampened. How would Jill react? When I got to Gallery Elite, Jill was already in the office. I was braced for drama. I thought she'd blame me for twisting Julius's arm, but I was wrong.

'They aren't all that bad. To be honest, I was surprised. If it really keeps him off the booze, we've got to do it.'

'I didn't know whether Julius had spoken to you about this.'

'Oh, you've made a hit there. He's eating out of your hand and even Marion seems to like you in her odd way. She seems so relieved to be free of the ARW site that she isn't rubbishing your drafts, which is amazing.'

'Great. So you actually like Baz's paintings?'

'I wouldn't go that far. They're much better than I expected. And Julius and I needed to get him into our tent a bit more. Personally I find my brother a pain, but cutting him out pushes him towards Sean -- and at the moment Sean's the bigger problem. He wants more money and more control -- and for some reason the Africa charity drives him mad.'

'Because ARW gets most of the funds?'

'I suppose that's it. Sean's totally selfish. Anyway, I've got a new idea for you, which I hope you'll like.'

This sounded promising. I was always drawn to new ideas.

'You're making a great start on the ARW site, so how would you like to take over the Gallery Elite site as well?'

'Wow! But what about Sean? It's his baby. I couldn't work with him. I mean I've got a lot of design ideas and some experience with Dreamweaver. You're not thinking that I do the design and he codes it up, are you?'

'No -- I was thinking that you'd take it over completely. Sean and I were talking about the site and I was a bit pushy. I came out with your phrase 'sense of audience', which he thinks is silly jargon. And I said things like the site has to be a work of art in itself, which he also thinks is nonsense. So we ended up having a row. Then he just refused to have anything more to do with it.'

'I'm surprised. I thought he was quite acquisitive about the business and controlling the website is part of that.'

'It's the cash he wants. I think the web site bores him. He soon picked up that I wanted to give it to you and he said you're welcome to it. The two of you looked at it together, didn't you?'

My heart sank, 'Yes but nothing came of that. Nothing happened really.'

'Well that's all right. He was quite rude about you actually – kept saying...well he was rather rude anyway. You've obviously rubbed him up the wrong way. I told him he was talking nonsense. Well, I had to say something. So the question is -- are you interested in taking on board the Gallery Elite site as well as the ARW site? It's a lot to ask. I think you've got the time.....but what's your reaction?'

Looking back, I didn't think much at all. I had the time in the gallery and a website about art really excited me.

'Jill, I'd absolutely love to develop the gallery site,

as long as I don't have to work with Sean.'

So it was done. In a couple of days, he sent me the username and password for the site host along with a rather snide message which I ignored – then the Gallery Elite site was my baby. To create a site which is itself a work of art, was a dream challenge I relished. I was not going to adapt Sean's flashy design. In any case it was written in code completely beyond me – so a fresh start was needed. I found a handful of gorgeous looking art sites from which I drew ideas. My head was full of colour flow, balance, subtlety, continuity, sense of audience. I had to use images of some of the pieces hanging in the gallery. With some cropping and photoshop tweaking, I managed to contrive some good images – and I made a point of including one of Baz's paintings.

One difficulty was that the overall purpose of the site was twofold. We didn't want people flocking to Gallery Elite then writing nasty reviews, so I weighted the site to the art consultancy. We wanted to attract potential purchasers to the consultancy with hints of more flexible methods than in the conventional art market. Jill was good with phrases like 'refreshing new insights', 'we do the research', 'the visual world is yours'.

At that point, I was so thrilled by the new challenge that I never considered that this was another step downwards.

24

My work life now became much busier, which was a great relief. The two web sites were not small undertakings, especially making the Gallery Elite site into 'a work of art'. In addition, every few days I did an art consultancy visit, rather similar to the visit to the doctor who wanted the Kandinsky for her father. These visits were diverse but I was becoming more confident and beginning to read the clients better. Jill always debriefed me and generally took over the client from me, but occasionally I was allowed to follow through to obtaining a print or even bidding at an auction.

Looking back, I didn't see Jill objectively. I saw her through the prism of my lost mother – and as a professional role model – and as someone who was bringing freedom to Suzan and Olivette in Africa. I especially identified with her determination to give those African girls a chance in life; that made me forgive her for all the bad acts she might have committed. Then of course, getting my Grandfather out of the hole, the threats; that was important. I somehow forgot the little fact that she had triggered his attempted purchase – and did it behind my back. I knew that in compromising, in not going to the police, I'd done wrong, but I could not risk incriminating my Grandfather. It was wrong morally, but overall, I had to live by my decision, for I had no better one. You have to choose the light over the dark, but sometimes it's not that simple. I kept the resignation option in reserve. The truth is that there was so much of interest going on, that it was easier to postpone the

move. I believed I would do it one day soon, but not
today. At that stage I was slipping into deeper waters
without realising it.

Tariq was too ill to work more than a day or
two a week and the condition came in bursts. I was
brought in to do more initial client interviews, several
a month; this with the development of the two web
sites, filled my time and kept me happier. The aim of
the initial interview was to ascertain the sort and level
of purchase likely to emerge and to develop trust
in me and enthusiasm for the process. I then would
brief Jill about the interview; she would then decide
if she would take it over or if it could be left with me.
Obviously I would only be left with the cheaper end of
the market; anything else was taken out of my hands.
And any client like my Grandfather, who wanted an
original and couldn't pay the market price, was taken
over by Jill.
Most of the clients I was allowed to hang on to
were interested in high quality photographic copies
of great paintings and in some cases painted copies.
These weren't forgeries as we were not pretending
they were the originals, and what the client then
chose to do with a painted copy was not our business.
We had a handful of skilled copyists on our books.
With some clients, it was not clear at first where
their interests lay, or how much funding they could
access. I found myself talking more and more openly
with Jill about the status and probable trajectory of
a client, to use her language. Early on, as agreed, I
did not know and was not told about any trajectory
which could result in theft, but as we became used
to working together and discussing clients, so the
barriers started to fade. 'Lifting an original' was her

language for stealing and this phrase started to drift into our discussions. I was not going to get directly involved in theft, but I knew one took place every few months and I often had met the client for the initial interview.

Officially I knew nothing about any theft, though if police had become involved, it would be difficult to maintain this fiction. Knowing about impending thefts became normal and I didn't worry about it too much. I had become part of the gang. It was only short term; Jill and Julius had both said that. We just had to get funds out to support the girls in Africa, and avoid getting caught out.

'Sadie, I need you to cover for me one day next week? Is that OK?'

'Yes, sure.'

'The Simpsons will be an easy couple to deal with. The trouble is I know him, knew him anyway. We were close actually, until I discovered he was married. This was way before Tariq and I met. I didn't realise that this was the John Simpson I was involved with and now, I can't possibly face him, and definitely not his wife.'

'Isn't that the couple in Dorking with the Kandinsky that the doctor is interested in?'

'Yes, that's right...'

'So why do we need to visit them?'

'They've asked for a consultant visit. They must have something in mind to purchase. They're investors. They use art to make lots of money, money that ought to go to Africa.'

I suddenly understood, 'You're going to steal the Kandinsky. Is that it?'

'That decision is way off – and you know nothing about that. That's what we agreed, Sadie.'

'I know, but I still feel bad about it.'

'Look Sadie, you're just doing your job as an art consultant. Why should you feel bad? It's all positive. And it's marvellous for me that you really care about Africa ARW. You're part of the team.'

'Well, at a distance.'

'Sadie, you are. Please, please, just do this one. For me.'

The rational part of me said, be careful, but Jill needed my help and I wasn't to be directly involved in any theft. I didn't really choose, but somehow found myself saying, 'Alright, I'll do it.' It was as if someone else had answered for me. This someone else said it as lightly as brushing a crumb from a sleeve. I was so stupid.

'Great. You're marvellous, Sadie. It's next Wednesday…you'll find it interesting. I thought he was an art lover but he's just an investor; that's all he's interested in. I dumped him when I knew he was married. He was not too pleased.'

'So I'll be walking into a bit of your personal story….'

'Plus the wife. Oh, and there might be a telephone engineer poking around the house while you're there, but you know nothing about that, even if you recognize him…'

I froze. 'Oh no, not Sean? Please Jill…'

'He won't look like Sean. He's good at disguises.'

So that was it. I was to provide cover while Sean checked over access or security or something….

I tensed up, 'I don't think I can do this….'

'Of course you can. You've agreed to it now and

I've got no one else to turn to. You know nothing, so personally you're completely safe. I didn't want to mention Sean but if you recognized him through the disguise, you might, I don't know, scream or something. No, you wouldn't do that. Anyway you're safe, just innocently doing your job.'

'That's the problem. I'm not innocent. I know what's going on. And it's wrong.'

'Then giving a new life to those girls in Africa is also wrong.'

'You know I'm not saying that.'

'Well I don't know how to improve the life chances of those girls without depriving some rich investors of a chunk of their profit. And I don't think you do either. You just play dumb if you're ever questioned, which you won't be. Your Grandfather's safe. You enjoy working on the two web sites. It's Julius and I that are taking the risks.'

So that was it. My qualms were trivial compared with the new lives we were giving the African girls. From that point on, Jill had won me over. Legally and morally I knew I was doing wrong -- and I was trapped.

25

I knew that the briefing session at Julius's flat was going to be an ordeal. I arrived with Jill. His office-lounge was a large first floor room. The window along one wall looked out over a private lawn with a drive up one side, enclosed by a high wall. The room was comfortable and packed with images of his past. There was a poster of a Jack Vettriano painting. Or was it the real thing? Posters from exhibitions in his galleries, a framed OU degree certificate -- and a blown-up photo of two women posing on a glamorous night out. One of these was Jill. I guessed that the other was the girlfriend. The drinks bar was well equipped. No one was there but Julius.

He was in a mellow mood. He embraced us both with a tacky charm. I was one of the family, almost Jill's younger sister. He sat us down on one of his huge black leather sofas and sorted out wine for Jill, fruit juice for me.

'We're just waiting for Sean. He was dipping into some emails. He won't be long.'

I had been dreading meeting Sean again but at least with the others around, he would behave.

' Sadie -- you did brilliantly with that Doctor...' Julius beamed at me. 'With any luck, she'll be giving her father the Kandinsky he wants in the final years of his life. Good on her. I wish all offspring were like that.'

I hesitated then, more sharply than I intended, came out with, 'I thought her father sounded a bit like my Grandfather ...'

'Ah. You might be right there. That still pains me, what Walter had to endure. Anyway, it's all over now, isn't it? And you're part of the team, which is good, especially given Tariq's....whatever it is....'

'He'll be back in a day or two, Pop. He'll be OK for the actual lift.'

'I believe you darling; thousands wouldn't. Now where's Sean?'

I was feeling very uncomfortable. I felt I had been dragged right into the centre of planning a theft when the agreement was that I should stay on the edge and officially 'know nothing'.

Jill murmured to me, 'Don't worry -- it'll be fine. I promise.'

After another pause, Julius said with some irritation, 'Sean should have sorted that stuff by now. Ah - here he is, right on cue.'

Sean swept in, with his usual athletic grace and a wave to all. He half smiled and raised a questioning eyebrow towards me.

Julius asked, 'How did the emails go?'

'One done, one to go. I'm not late, am I? Well, if it isn't young Sadie. So you've been dragged into the kingdom of evil...'

His playful tone was hard to match, but Jill shielded me, '...of virtue, Sean, if only you could see it.'

He looked sideways at me and said knowingly, 'Virtue? I see...'

I cringed. He turned to Julius, 'So Sadie's filling in while Tariq's on his happy pills....alright. So what's the programme?'

'The programme? Yes -- to business. First I've got some copies of the house plan where the painting is. Sadie, they're just behind you. Give them out will you, there's a dear. The house owners are John and

Estelle Simpson.'

I had no choice, the new girl, the junior.

Julius waited till I'd finished. 'Alright? As you can see, it's a large detached house. I've marked the painting on the downstairs plan. It's in the back room off the hall.' He paused while we examined it.

'Sean is going in as a telephone engineer, to check out security. When he's in, Sadie will call, by appointment, to tell them about some paintings which are coming on to the market. You'll be there as a distraction Sadie, so Sean is free to poke around. We haven't decided when we're going to lift the painting yet. First we need to know exactly what security they've got.'

My God! I'm there as a distraction. But I meekly said, 'So….what paintings am I telling them about?'

Jill jumped in. 'That's all sorted. I've got images of eight or nine paintings from the Kandinsky period, and some of those really are on the market. You can pretend you have advance notice of the others. So if anyone goes on the web, they can find enough confirmation of what you said. We'll rehearse the whole thing before you go in.'

Julius continued, 'Your appointment Sadie is for five pm on Wednesday at the Simpson house. You're a professional consultant working with the Gallery Peerless. OK?'

'Gallery Peerless? But what about Gallery Elite?'

There was silence. Sean rolled his eyes at my stupidity.

Julius winked at me. 'It's OK dear. We're just building a little story for the Simpsons. We don't want them to come calling. Right?'

I winced. I was really in it now.

Julius turned to Sean. 'You will arrive at four fifty,

in your BT work gear. The usual story; some incoming calls have been lost. You need to check the telephone connections or they risk being cut off from the world. Brian will bring a Telecoms van round to you at around three and collect it again around seven.'

Sean nodded. 'That's fine. How recent are these plans?'

'The house changed hands two years ago and I got loads of bumph from some estate agent friends of mine, so recent enough.'

'And how do we know the painting is right there, in that room?'

'I got a friend of mine to chat up their window cleaner.'

Jill said, 'Leonie?'

'Amazing what a well-turned out woman can do...'

I glanced up at the photo of the woman with Jill. Julius saw this and winked at me.

He said to Sean, 'And there are security cameras around...'

'That's no surprise....so I keep away from the painting room until Sadie has....got the couple's full attention...'

'You've got it. Apart from John and Estelle, there's a housekeeper. She's a danger, but with luck she'll be busy making a meal or something. We'll have to trust to luck there.'

Jill said, 'What about disguises? I've got stuff for Sadie....'

This was a shock. I'd forgotten. I blurted out, 'Disguises? Is that necessary.....' -- then dried up.

Sean turned on me. 'Of course it's bloody well necessary. After we lift the painting, the police are going to want to know who's been near that security system, and they'll have the video footage. I don't know about you Sadie, but as far as I'm concerned, the images of me are definitely not going to look like this.'

He framed his face in my direction.

Jill snapped out. 'Leave her alone Sean. She's just starting out.'

'It's risky enough as it is without pulling in a beginner…'

I felt like running away but just stood there, blushing.

Julius opened his arms in my direction. 'It's alright my dear. Worry not. Jill has a disguise ready for you and Sean has set up a website for that famous virtual gallery, the Peerless as cover. You're Marina Ward, art consultant. You'll have to familiarise yourself with the site. It'll vanish immediately before the painting is lifted. And so will Marina Ward.'

I was struggling to cope with all this, on top of Sean's outburst, 'Marina Ward - right. Yes, I understand now…'

Julius smiled, Of course you do. And Marina Ward will vanish into thin air, as if by magic.'

Jill put an encouraging hand on my shoulder. 'We've got some stuff ready for you -- and a gorgeous wig. You won't recognise yourself. I promise you.'

I just kept silent, tried to look cool. Was it too late to back out? I couldn't answer. My mind had seized up.

'Good. Are we finished? Sean, have you got anything out of the emails yet?'

'I've only got into Estelle's so far; nothing much really. She's having an affair. That might be useful. And it looks like they'll both be at home on Wednesday afternoon.'

So he was hacking into the emails of the owners of the Kandinsky. I saw Jill straighten on hearing of the wife's affair.

'I'm working on the husband's email now. That might tell me what security firm they used. That could be useful - and there might be other secrets to winkle out.'

I should never have got anywhere near this man. I thought back to when he glided into the gallery and copied something from the filing cabinet. He'd said -- no need to let Jill know; I fell for it like a fool. Then the sexual approaches -- and the voice on Walter's phone. He was clever and manipulative. I felt vengeful and very vulnerable. And I was trapped into working with him to fool this Simpson couple.

'Right everyone. That's it for today. We'll meet here on Thursday, same time, see what you've found out.'

Jill murmured to me, 'I'm staying to have a chat with Julius. It's too late to open the gallery again today. See you tomorrow.'

I had little choice to follow Sean out of the flat. He held the lift back for me and waved me in. I ignored him and walked to the stairs.

I heard him call out, 'Please yourself.'

Childish perhaps, but I was never getting into any enclosed space with that man.

26

A day or two later, Jill got me ready for being the 'distraction' at the Simpsons. I was slightly more composed about it all, and tried to think of it as more of a challenge than an ordeal. We shut the gallery early and Jill drove us round to her flat. There was no sign of Harry or Tariq.

'Harry's gone to a friend's house after play school; his social life is really stepping up.'

The room was much tidier than when I baby sat. On the living room table, Jill had placed a laptop and various items in tempting gift boxes.

'You have a look at that lot Sadie, while I check that Tariq is OK.'

The first box I opened held a wig -- a fearsome reddish-brown mop. In the next there was a high necked and belted dark blue dress and some black pants. In the final was a pair of navy platform shoes. It was exciting getting all these together. Jill knew exactly what worked well on me. I could hardly wait to try them on. That is except for the wig.

She came back, 'Tariq's not too bad. He's dozing and watching TV. He'll come through later when you're all rigged out to give you a once over.'

That I did not want, but then it was nothing to what I was to face at the Simpsons.

Jill opened up the laptop and said, 'Let's start on the script. The usual stuff really except it's tuned to their particular interests, his interests anyway. As far as I know she hasn't got any.'

'Have you met her?'

'No. And I don't want to. That's why you're involved remember? Now look at these. John has some very splendid and valuable Bauhaus paintings and he's after more. I've got about a dozen images here, half of which are on the market now. The other half aren't, but might be some time, such as this Klee -- and this Mondrian. That's to tantalise him. I've assembled notes for you on where they are and some guideline prices. Your line is this -- for those that aren't on the market, we have some behind-the-scenes intelligence and contacts. Right?'

They were beautiful images, some of them ravishing. The idea of trying to sell these glorious creations was strangely exciting, except that it wasn't for real.

'Why don't I let you browse through the pictures and the notes, then we can have a little run through when I've got you dressed up? Meanwhile I'll get us some coffee and cake ...'

I knew a lot about the Bauhaus movement from my uni course and I had seen most of the paintings, at least photos of them. It was about ten minutes before Jill returned with the coffee. She must have looked in on Tariq.

'Here we are. Help yourself ... so have you had a look at the clothes and a wig? What did you think?'

I munched some fruit cake then said, 'The clothes are great but the wig is horrific.'

'I know. But it will change the shape of your face and if ever the security video is examined, you'll be safe. It's as simple as that. You sacrifice vanity for security. In this game Sadie, security is all.'

'I guess you're right. I'll just have to swallow hard and avoid mirrors.'

'Right, so why don't you slip these things on. And

we'll leave the wig to the end.'

I started with the clothes and Marina Ward emerged. They felt great, even the platforms.

'You look terrific Sadie. Those heels really do something for you. Now let's get this wig on.'

It was quite close to the colour of my own hair but it seemed to sprout out in all directions and came close around my face, shrinking it. The effect was to make me look bigger, more dominant, more alternative, but with a small face.

'That's good, very good. It doesn't look like you at all.'

I fiddled with the wig to try to feel less strapped in, but with no success. I felt clamped in a hairy rug.

'Now Sadie, I mean Marina, sit down on the sofa with your laptop and prepare to give Tariq a demo. That's what he's waiting for. He's playing John Simpson, heaven help us.'

Jill went to the hallway and shouted, 'Tariq, there's an art consultant here come to try to interest you in some new paintings.'

This was not just silly play-acting. If I was going to do this, I had to do it well. I sat down on the sofa and adopted a pose.

From the bedroom Tariq shouted that he was on his way and in a few moments he appeared in a black dressing gown. He looked a bit spaced out.

He said, 'Hello there. Nice to meet you, Marina.' His speech was slightly slurred. 'I gather you've got some interesting pictures to show me. Alright if I sit beside you here?'

So we were doing the role-play thing, but it was good experience. They sat on either side of me and quizzed me about my new gallery, the Peerless. Then

I showed the images -- and they quizzed me more. I think we all did rather well playing our parts.

At last Tariq said, 'Stop. I can't take any more. Sadie, you're brilliant. You're a natural. I'd buy the lot if I had the cash.'
Jill said, 'No you wouldn't. It would all go to Africa. Anyway this little exercise should raise enough to build another school, so we've got to get it right. But she's done well, hasn't she?'
Tariq nodded. The encounter seemed to have exhausted him and he had to go back to his bedroom.
I removed my mop wig and got into my own clothes.
'So you're ready. Just remember -- if you see Sean, don't react. He's a telecoms engineer and a total stranger to you.'
'I know. I'll be careful. Is Harry back soon?'

I really wanted to stay till Harry returned, but Jill said he'd be an age, so I left for the nearby tube station, with the laptop in one hand and the Marina clothes and wig nicely packed in a bag in the other -- and a reluctant determination that I was just going to have to get through this.

I was thinking back to when the three of us were sitting together in a pub with my phone on the table. That was when they had been forced to make some shocking revelations about how the African charity was funded. Now I was part of their game.

27

I parked well along the road from the Simpson house, so that I could take full control of myself and get the feel of the place as I approached. It was a handsome three-storey town house, wide fronted at the base and becoming narrower as it ascended, almost pyramid like. The front was covered with shuttered windows, was well maintained and reeked of wealth. On the drive, outside the front door, was a Telecoms van.

I felt awkward. My wig was itchy and hot. Trussed up in a high necked and tightly belted dress might look great over black pants and platform shoes -- but Grandfather's phrase of 'mutton dressed up as lamb' came to me.

I was clutching a briefcase which held my laptop with the images of the paintings. I had rehearsed the script carefully. Walking up steps to the front door in the platform shoes was awkward.

The front door was opened by a rather tall, well groomed woman in her forties.

'Hi. You must be the gallery person, Marina isn't it? I'm Estelle Simpson...'

She smiled warmly, which was a relief -- and ushered me into the hall.

'It's John who's interested in the paintings, but I might sit in with you.'

I took in the costly billowing haircut and the possible facelift. She looked as if she was in preparation for some very special event. Her hair, skin and clothes glowed with expensive care. I was quite drawn to her.

162

She led the way. 'I think he's in here. We're hoping you've got some really interesting stuff to show us.'

In the large light room, there were two huge sofas and flamboyant lime green patterned curtains. On the wall facing the fireplace were two commanding early 20th century paintings.

'John, this is Marina from Gallery -- what is it again?'

'Peerless.'

'Peerless. Of course.'

John bounced to his feet and shook my hand.

'Hi there Marina. I must visit your gallery some day....'

He looked younger than his wife -- and less formally dressed in black shirt and jeans. He had a rather large square face, balding and very red lips. It was hard to believe that Jill and he were so close but I could see what she saw in him.

I gulped and said, 'We're only a small gallery and mostly focus on outside consultancy, which is why I'm here.'

'Good. Well, look around and you can see what I'm keen on, mainly the Blue Four, but not only them.'

I recognised the paintings in the room and moved to look at them more closely.

'This is a late Jawlenski, isn't it? I absolutely love it.'

'Sounds like you've a kindred spirit here, darling.'

'Yes it's a fine painting and let me tell you something else about it. It's increased in value by more than fifty percent in the three years I've owned it.'

'Wow, that is amazing.'

'It's a real win-win. I've got something good for

the wall, though not all our guests seem to agree. And when I sell it, the profit margin is even more beautiful, but you must know all about that.'

'Of course. Played cleverly, the art market is so much better than the housing market.'

'Agreed. But we need specialist knowledge. I guess I know a fair bit, as you can judge from these beauties'. He leaned a little towards me and murmured, 'But it might help to have you on my side.'

After a slightly uncomfortable pause, Estelle said, 'So you work out of Gallery Peerless. We've never heard of that, have we John?'

John said nothing but looked quizzically at me... and I had my script.

'We're new, that's why and we're largely virtual. I work semi-independently out of Peerless and have a number of clients for whom I seek items on or near the market. I like to think that we have good intelligence, so we know what's coming up before it gets there -- and sometimes there are great advantages for clients in that. Can I show you a few pictures?'

We sat down on a long sofa. I manoeuvred my laptop out of the briefcase on to my knee. They sat either side of me and I started showing the images of some paintings cunningly selected by Jill.

I fell back on my learned lines and was relieved to see John Simpson engrossed. His knowledge of the art market was good.

'These are very interesting, Marina. Wow -- I'd love that.'

'Don't go mad darling. We're after investments here...'

'Let me see the previous one again -- the Klee, yes that one. Surely that's in the large gallery in

Hamburg. I've seen it. They're never going to sell that, surely?'

'Well that's the intelligence we've picked up. We might be wrong. I can explore further and let you know.'

I quaked, but he swallowed it. After all, I was the expert, wasn't I?

Quite suddenly the door swung open and someone peered into the room. The head didn't look at all like Sean. He now had a fine head of dark hair and some rather cool specs. But when he entered, his build and grace even with overalls and a bag of kit, was unmistakable. I froze.

He glanced at me then turned to John and spoke in a deep cockney voice, 'Oh sor-ree. I thought there might be a phone in here.'

Estelle jumped up and said sharply, 'There is but we're busy right now. I thought Mary was looking after you ...I'd better sort this out. Just come with me please...'

'No, hang on Estelle. If this chap has to look at this phone, why don't I show Marina the Kandinsky?' To Sean he said, 'How long do you need in here, mate?'

'Five minutes max...'

'That's ideal.'

John ushered me out of the room. Estelle stayed put, perhaps to keep an eye on the BT Engineer.

I followed John into the room at the back of the house, but of course I could have shown him the route as I knew the house plan.

The Kandinsky completely dominated the large otherwise empty room. I felt overwhelmed, almost in a state of shock; being so close to this extraordinary painting. It was more than six foot wide and four high. There was so much bewildering almost garish detail grabbing the eye and sending it off into another and yet another weird construction. Meaning? Impossible to say. Just gorgeously beautiful.

He gave me a couple of minutes to take it in. 'Like it?'

'Oh -- it's wonderful. Overwhelming. I want to stay here for ever...'

'I'm sure we can arrange something, but not quite for ever...'

'Sorry. I'm so excited..'

'I can tell that. I think the telephone guy might be done by now. And don't we need to look at the rest of your pictures?"

Estelle met us in the hall. 'That guy's been all over the place. I suppose you just have to trust these people. I told Mary to keep an eye on him but he's had her making coffee for him. ...'

'Don't worry dear. He'll have seen the cameras.'

'Yes. He was taking a good look at them.' She turned to me, 'Sorry about that, Marina. Security can be a nightmare. You must know all about that.'

'Well, a little. I've read about art thefts ...' I almost choked at my stupidity, but managed, 'They seem fairly rare -- and you've got cameras and other systems in place, haven't you?'

'We certainly have. I was in software earlier and I know a thing or two about security.'

I thought -- these are clever people. Do they believe a word I say?

'I think I've shown you most of the images. I've just a few more....'

Estelle said, 'Oh good. Can we start at the beginning again?'

'If you're both happy with that...'

'Yes, quickly. I want Estelle to see that Klee.'

I showed the sequence of images again. Some of them were exquisite. John reaffirmed his interest in the Klee, which I knew was definitely not for sale, but I had a price range.

Estelle had a firmer approach. 'That's fine but I'd need to know the likely rate of appreciation. John's the art lover. I'm the investor.'

'It's only the Klee I'm interested in. Keep us up to speed about what's happening there. Is it really coming on the market? Where and when? Can you negotiate privately for us?'

I thought, mission accomplished, 'We can certainly explore that. We should be able to get some details within a few weeks. We'll contact you when we have something...'

John walked me to the door, a little too closely for my liking, but using personal charms to fix a deal was part of my new profession.

'This has been so interesting, Marina. I'm really looking forward to hearing from you very soon.'

He shook my hand then gave me a little hug. I thought, you're more Jill's type than mine.

Outside the house, the Telecoms van had gone.

It was a vast relief to be walking back to the rental car. I'd managed the visit rather well, except when Sean came into the room. I hoped that John Simpson didn't read anything into my discomfort.

After a few blocks drive I felt safe enough to pull off the wig and begin to feel like myself again. This was a real sense of achievement, to be set against all the deceit.

I ducked out of the 'reporting back to Julius' session. Walter was unwell so I had an excuse. I simply told Jill what had happened. It was Sean who had the critical information, and I was relieved to be able to avoid another session with him in Julius's lounge.

28

On the day of the Kandinsky theft, I was in the gallery as usual. Sean and Tariq were 'lifting' the painting. Possibly Kyle as well? Jill was trying to work on the Africa project in the back office. She was very edgy, couldn't sit still, just waiting for news.

She kept popping into the gallery, babbling things like, 'Tariq'll text me when they're back in Julius's flat, he always does. I get a bit scared – in case something goes wrong.'

Her fear was contagious, but I tried to support her. 'Everything's planned Jill ... and Sean seems on top of all the security stuff.'

Hypocrite, I thought to myself, praising that bastard to calm down Jill.

'You're right -- it's the tension. I mean if something went wrong and Tariq was caught, arrested or something, that would be the end. What would Harry and I do? And if I was taken away too, which I would be, I can't bear to think about what would happen to Harry ...'

I sat thinking, have you never realised this before? I thought about Harry; obviously he couldn't go to Jill's parents. What about Tariq's parents? What about me? But I said nothing...

Jill's mobile rang in the office. She ran in.

'WHAT?' She almost screamed. 'What's happened, Pop? Where's Tariq?'

I rushed into the office to face Jill wide-eyed and staring, She gasped out, 'It's off! I don't know what's happened but it's off. I've got to go to Julius's. Come with me, Sadie.'

'Where's Tariq?'

'He's there with Julius. Something's gone wrong. Julius is in a state...'

We closed up the gallery more or less -- and Jill drove us to Julius's flat. Her driving terrified me; I just held on to the seat. It was raining, she took risks with lights. She swore at anything in the way.

We ignored the lift and ran upstairs as quickly as our lungs allowed. The flat door was open. Julius was pacing backwards and forwards.

Julius snarled, 'At last. I thought you'd never be here.'

'Pop, what the hell is going on?'

Tariq was standing staring fixedly out of the window. He didn't seem to register our arrival at all.

Julius bellowed, 'Haven't you seen the news? The bloody painting's been stolen. It's vanished!'

'What do you mean? I don't know what you're talking about. Tell me what's happened.'

He spoke to Jill as if she was a stupid child. 'The painting that Sean and Tariq were going to lift today, was stolen by somebody else yesterday. So it's not there for us. Get it? Look at this.'

He almost threw the local paper at Jill. The headline was PRICELESS PAINTING STOLEN FROM MANSION. The theft had taken place on the previous evening.

Jill and I skimmed the article. Jill said, 'I don't believe this. It *is* the same painting.'

Julius snapped at her, 'Of course it's the same bloody painting....'

Tariq just stared down at the garden in a sort of trance, but I don't think his eyes registered the private lawn, the narrow drive or the high wall. For myself, I was an outsider to all this raging, the nervous observer.

Jill asked pointedly, 'Where's Sean?'

'Heaven knows. I left him a message when I rang you. He didn't answer. Damn! You're right. It's him isn't it. Playing his bloody stupid games.'

Jill said, 'It could be. Tariq, you're supposed to be with him. What the hell are you doing here?'

Tariq was dragged out of his trance. He was tetchy, 'We were supposed to be doing a job today. That's all I know.'

Jill shouted at him, 'Why the hell are you here and not with Sean?' I'd never heard her like that with him.

Poor guy -- he looked wretched. He was almost pleading, 'He was going to pick me up -- nothing happened. I rang him again and again, then Julius called me. So I came here. That's it.'

Julius, who was standing repeatedly batting a fist into his other hand, barked out, 'Of course I called you. Sean wasn't bloody answering and I wanted to know what the hell was going on...'

Tariq turned towards the window again, as if he was alone. He gave no response.

Jill was ashen. 'So what the hell do we do now?'

Nobody seemed to know what to do. Julius paced back and forth. Jill slumped and fiddled with her hair. I just leaned against the wall.

Tariq was still looking out of the window on to the parking area, then his body suddenly jerked. I followed his eyes and saw that the roller door to the lane was being opened.

My heart sank as I saw who it was. 'Somebody's coming in.' I couldn't bear to name him.

Jill rushed to the window, 'It's Kyle. God. That's Sean's van. He's driving in.'

I moved over to the large window and watched the white van back on to the drive, then Kyle shut the large roller door. The van backed right up to the rear door, then Sean jumped out. I felt slightly sick at seeing Kyle with Sean. He had said he was getting out of Sean's life. I thought again of my messing up with Sean.

Somebody else clambered out of the van passenger door.

Julius snarled, 'What the bloody hell is Baz doing here?'

I had the image of hyper-fit Sean on the floor exercising inside Baz's flat, then Eva's talk of plotting.

Sean and Kyle opened the rear doors of the van. Baz stood smugly watching. He looked up to our window, long enough to check he was observed, smirked then followed Kyle into the back of the van.

Sean pressed the intercom. Julius grabbed the handset and bellowed, 'What the hell are you up to this time?'

We could all hear Sean's reply. He was pointedly casual, 'Hi Julius. Sorry I'm a bit late. I've got something for you.' Sean looked up. Eventually Julius had to press the door release. Sean gave a thumbs-up.

Jill said, 'God -- doesn't he just love himself?'

Sean jumped into the back of the van, then Kyle appeared moving backwards, struggling with one end of a heavy burden. A large painting covered by a white cloth was eased out of the van. It was six foot long and very heavy. Kyle at one end, came first, using a strap with handles to support the awkward load. Baz was next holding the painting upright. Sean was last with a strap holding the other end.

Julius shouted, 'They've got the painting. They've got the bloody painting. I'm going to murder that Sean.' He was red and panting with anger. 'What the hell is he playing at? We had the whole thing planned out for today... Tariq, did you know about this?'

Tariq was indignant, 'No. Nothing. I was waiting for him to pick me up -- that was the plan....'

He looked wretched and I saw Jill staring at him.

Julius also looked in a bad state, panting, clutching his chest. Was he having a heart attack? I tried to recall my first aid. Jill went to his side and tried to support him.

'Pop, we're just going to have to cope with this. Calm down. Don't do anything stupid.'

Julius shrugged her off, opened the flat door and went on to the landing, followed by the rest of us. Jill put her fingers to her lips, perhaps to calm her father. We could hear the men carrying the heavy painting into the lift, then the whirring motor, jerking to a halt. The doors opened to reveal the painting covered by a large cloth, Sean and Kyle at either side, Baz standing behind it. Julius and Jill, at the front, blocked the two men from moving, while Tariq and I stood well behind them.

Julius hissed at Sean, 'What the hell are you at? You bloody imbecile. ...'

Sean shrugged and smirked a little. 'I just thought I'd save you a few hours work. That's all....'

Nobody moved. No one knew what to do.

Then Sean said with mock casualness, 'We could just leave this beauty here, but it seems a shame.....'

Julius and Jill had to move aside. Sean and Kyle struggled to move the painting with Baz in the middle. Tariq made no move to help. He just backed into the lounge -- he looked as if he was in a stupor.

They manhandled the covered painting into Julius's lounge, then lent it against the back of the sofa.

Julius, very red, shouted, 'Sean, what the hell are you playing at?'

Sean glanced at him then said quietly, 'Taking a bit more control, like I said I would.'

Suddenly Julius launched himself at Sean and grabbed his throat. Jill, Kyle and I rushed to restrain him.

Jill shouted, 'Pop. Stop it. What are you doing?'

Julius shouted, 'Murdering him -- what do you think?' He shrugged off our restraining arms, then slumped into a chair, panting and exhausted. Sean gestured as if to say -- silly man.

Jill, glaring at Baz, snarled, 'And why the hell is he here?'

Sean spoke calmly as if nothing had happened. 'Simple. Baz is keen to get involved in the family business -- and Tariq's still on happy pills....'

Tariq who had been silent, looked desperate, then lurched himself towards Sean. He got very close then stopped short and whispered loud, 'At least I'm not a disgusting pervert...' and ran out of the room, weeping, or was it fury? I couldn't tell.

Jill ran after him. After a few moments, she returned alone.

I said to her, 'Shall I go after him?'

She ignored me and glared with fury at Sean, who said pointedly to her, 'Dear me. Something's really getting at him...'

'What the hell does that mean?'

Sean shrugged, 'You'd never guess....'

Then he signalled to Kyle to help him slowly draw back the cloth covering the painting.

Suddenly for me, everything changed. As the painting was revealed, I honestly gasped at the splendour of Kandinsky's genius. Being so near again, it had a bewildering power. Of course I had seen it at the Simpson's but having it resting on the floor, inches from me was like being close to a miracle. The wildness of the shapes, the power of the colours, hit me like jumping into a waterfall. It was like heaven and hell rolled into one.

Baz, drew back his hands, as if presenting the painting to an audience, 'Ladies and gentlemen, here you have it....'

Jill hissed at him, 'For heaven's sake, keep your stupid mouth shut!'

He curled his face up in mock terror.

I turned to find Kyle, behind me, quite close. He winked at me. I blanked him. I wanted no contact.

Julius was sitting back, panting and speaking in jerks, 'He needs to tell us -- what the hell he's -- playing at.'

Jill barked out,- 'Sean. Explain. Why have you done this?'

'It's quite simple. I've been through it with Julius, again and again and again.'

Julius panted, 'Not that fucking -- rubbish. We're a team. We've got a -- system that works'

'It might work for you, but for me, it's no good. You're past it Julius. I sorted out the security system, like I do with every job. Kyle and I lifted the painting, with some help from Baz. We're the new team. We don't need you any more. Your so-called system wouldn't work without my skills -- and you haven't got anybody else to do the job. I get a paltry ten percent of the takings. I ought to get half -- and I'm going to in future.'

There was silence, apart from Julius's breathing.

'Next, this Africa farce. It's a stupid waste of money. A drop in the ocean might make you feel good, Jill. It does damn all for Africa.'

I'd heard that 'drop in the ocean' phrase before from Kyle, who I wanted to slap.

Jill was furious, 'That's nonsense. You're talking total crap!'

Sean rested a hand possessively on the frame of the painting. 'You know I sometimes think that Baz is the only sane member of your family.'

Jill launched herself at Sean and Baz, 'Sane? Him? Don't be stupid. What you can't see is that the cash has given a future to dozens of young girls, people who are just as important as you are, more, they're decent. You've got no conscience; you don't care about anyone else. If it wasn't for the African project, I wouldn't be involved, nor would Julius. It just wouldn't happen and you wouldn't get your ten percent. Alright, you've got your skills, but what about the sounding out of the market, the initial contacts. What about Sadie covering for you while you did your security stuff? You think Baz could have managed that?'

I felt completely helpless. There was nothing I could do. I just stood with my back to the wall. Julius was still red and panting; I was frightened for him.

Sean said quietly, 'Jill, if I jump ship, you're lost.'

Baz nodded with glee towards his sister.

'But fear not, I'm not going to, provided you agree to my changes. Here's how it's going to be. From now on half the cash is coming to me. You can do what the hell you want with the rest. You can keep your Africa nonsense going if you want to, but at a low level.'

Julius panted out, 'Half? You're mad....you're a greedy -- fucking bastard.'

Sean shrugged and seemed untouched by the anger around him.

'I know you and Jill won't agree right away so you're just going to think about it for a couple of days. But there's one thing you can be certain of. If you refuse, I'll leave your little team and shop you to the police. And I'll vanish. I've done it before and I'll do it again. You see, I don't think you've a lot of choice.'

Baz added, 'That's right. Look guys, we need Sean on board.' Everyone ignored him.

There was a long silence, apart from Julius's breathing. He was in a bad state. He was panting and holding his chest.

Sean, cool as ever, added, 'Tariq will go along with it; you can be sure of that. Sadie's hardly in the team yet. Julius is past it. So it's really up to you, Jill. If you want to keep any of your Africa thing going, you're going to accept my terms. And if you decide there's no deal, you'd better prepare for the law.'

He moved towards the door followed by Baz, then Kyle, who gave a glance in my direction. I looked away.

'I'm going to leave this painting with you because you're going to agree. You've no choice.'

They went out, leaving the door open. We could hear them going down the stairs, Baz babbling on, part of the team.

Julius remained sitting, staring into space.

Jill kept saying to herself, 'Oh God. What a mess...'

I just stood. I had nothing to say. I was still entranced by the Kandinsky. Then above the painting, I saw the three men climbing back into the white van which was eased out into the lane. Sean jumped out, glanced back at us before carefully shutting the drive doors. I thought, he could have left them open. Does he think he's gone too far?

No longer pinned down, Jill turned to her father, 'Pop, I think we'd better get you to a doctor. Or what about A&E? We need to see what's going on...'

'Stuff A&E. There's some heart pills somewhere. That's all I need. In the bathroom.'

I said, 'I'll get them...' and we moved into our old roles again, as if Sean's arrival and his threats had been a bad dream.

But the miraculous painting now dominated Julius's living room -- everything had changed.

After he'd taken the pills, Julius started recovering. Jill sat down near him and patted his hand talked quietly to him. I felt in the way so left and made my way home.

When I finally reached the flat, Mel was busy in the kitchen. After this afternoon, I was finding it harder and harder to pretend that nothing was going on. At least Kyle was not around, thank God.

29

Next day back in the gallery, Jill came in with news that surprised me. Her father was on the mend and Sean had backed down. What 'backed down' meant was that Sean would get a third of the takings and they'd agreed to it. That was still a vast increase on ten percent. The fifty percent threat had been a bargaining stance. He'd fooled Julius and Jill with it. In any case, it meant less cash was available for Africa.

When I got home, Kyle was there cooking. I didn't want to see him, but acted normal for Mel's sake. I'd had fun with the first Kyle -- the friendly, uncomplicated, brother of my best friend. I couldn't handle this other Kyle, living with Sean, presumably having sex with Sean, and then saying he wanted to get away from Sean. The one who'd come with Sean and Baz and the Kandinsky. Yet the two Kyles were one person. I couldn't cope with this.

Mel and Kyle were in the kitchen, Kyle at the stove. I could tell from the way he glanced at me that he was worried about what I might say. I was saying nothing. I didn't know what Mel knew and I didn't want to upset her.

After a while, Mel went off to get ready to go out. She was going for a drink with some work pals.

Kyle, turning from the stove, said to me, 'I need to talk with you...'

'I'm sure you do. What does Mel know?'

'Nothing and it's got to stay that way. Please Sadie...'

I was angry with him, but curious about what Sean was up to -- and shamefully I suppose, about their relationship.

'Alright, I'll listen to what you've got to say for yourself, nothing more.'

'Thanks Sadie. Mel's going out so, you know… later.'

That evening, Kyle's menu was fried burger and beans; at least he took his turn. We munched our way through his offering then Mel left. We turned to each other over the table of dirty dishes.

'Thank God, at last. I really need to talk to you.'

I looked him in the eye, 'Oh yes? About your partner?'

'I told you about all of that in the pub. He's not my partner. Look, I rent a room in his flat and I give him a hand now and then. It doesn't mean anything. Honestly.'

'But you were involved with him…..'

'A few months ago maybe, but he got sick of me. He says I'm immature. Well I can't help that, can I. And he has other blokes around…'

'Kyle, I don't want to know that.'

Then he gave me a long look and said rather bitterly, 'No, I'm sure you don't….'

He held my eyes and slightly raised an eyebrow. I realised that Sean had told him. I felt myself blushing and lowered my head.

He realised he'd offended me, 'It's alright Sadie, honestly. Nobody knows anything and I'm as silent as a grave…'

'But *you* know! And it's none of your business. What's he been saying to you? Come on -- out with it!'

'I know something happened. I don't know what and like you say, it's none of my business. Alright?'

'So what did he say? What exactly did Sean say to you?'

'Hardly anything. He said you'd been -- getting keen on him, but then rushed off. Something like that.'

He was trying to water down whatever Sean had said. He was pleading with me. It was difficult to think totally ill of him.

I glared at him and barked out, 'Don't you see how awful it is for me, nearly having sex with your boyfriend. It makes me sick.'

'Sadie, he's not my boyfriend. That's all in the past. I'm sorry'

'Just don't mention any of that stuff about Sean and me again -- ever. I was stupid and I don't want reminding....'

'Right. Sorry. I don't know what tact is. That's what Mel says. But I am trying...'

'Well try harder.'

'I will. Honestly. Look what I wanted to say is this. I've got to get away from Sean, out of his house...and Mel says I can stay here for a while. But it's your flat. Just for a few days, till I get somewhere else sorted.'

He was pleading, 'So can I? Please, Sadie.'

'Of course you can't. In any case, where would you sleep? There's only two bedrooms.'

'On the sofa, like when I stay the night. It won't be for long...Sean has blokes in -- and I can't stand it..'

'I see...you get jealous?'

'Maybe. Some blokes that you know.....'

'Oh?'

'They come for a massage, but it turns into something else.'

I stared at him. What now? 'Who? You'd better tell me...'

'Tariq. Sean's really got his claws into Tariq...'

'Jill's husband?'

'Yeah, that Tariq.'

Harry's dad? Jill's partner? 'I don't believe you.'

'It's true. Why do you think Tariq acted like he did when we brought the painting? Sean's using him. He's got some sort of control over him.'

'But Tariq's ill...he's depressed.'

'Of course he is. Sean's driving him mad. He's -- I don't know -- cast a spell on him or something...'

I felt like bursting out crying. This was too much.

I tried to calm myself, but my voice wavered, 'Why are you telling me this?'

'I don't want to upset you Sadie, but I have to tell someone and like I said, I trust you.'

'Alright. Why are you telling me or anybody for that matter?'

He was near tears himself, '....because you'll do something sensible...'

'Like what?'

'I don't know what. That's why I'm telling *you*.'

Facing this tearful guy over dirty dishes after a shoddy meal made me feel almost desperate. My mind was whirling; I was trying to get my head round all of this. He was telling me some awful stuff and expecting me to do something sensible.

'What do you mean – cast a spell? I don't understand you.'

'He's using Tariq to get control over the art thing. And he's mangling up Tariq's head. It's all wrong. Tariq's a decent guy.'

'But you've been helping him, stealing that last painting...'

'Well I was a bloody fool, wasn't I? I needed the money, that's all. I didn't want him to take me back or anything. He just tolerates me being around and that's it. Sadie, I can't take any more.'

'So now you're after revenge?'

Kyle looked anywhere but at me and murmured, 'Something like that. But that's not the main thing.'

I felt I was just starting to understand him, 'You want to use me like you claim Sean is using Tariq...'

'God no....I don't want to use you in any way. Honestly. I really like you Sadie. Alright then, I'll say it. I love you.'

'Kyle, don't be stupid. You don't mean that.'

He lowered his head on to his arms on the table. I couldn't see his face but I could tell he was miserable. He looked up, tearful.

'Alright, but I like you a lot, really Sadie. You've got to believe me.'

I said nothing.

'And I've got to tell someone. You're the only one I trust. I mean I can't talk to Jill. As far as she's concerned, I'm Sean's slave. And Julius is -- I don't know. In any case, if Sean knew I'd told anyone, I don't know what he'd do to me but it would be nasty. So what am I supposed to do?'

'You want to take revenge on Sean for rejecting you. Is that it?'

'No. That's not the whole thing, I promise you Sadie.'

He was pleading with me and moving towards tears.

'Look, I admit being dumped really hurt, but the main thing is what he's getting away with. He's out to get Jill.'

I stared at him.

'How?'

'He made Tariq get her email password so he

could, I don't know, see her secrets or something like that...'

'My God. That's vile, awful. How do you know that?'

'Don't ask me...I'm ashamed....'

'What? Tell me!'

'I came back early one time and his bedroom door wasn't tight closed, so I listened to them.'

'Oh Kyle, that's awful. So what now? What can we do?'

'I honestly don't know. Stop Sean from taking over...'

Kyle and I spent a while longer anguishing over this. He didn't know that my Grandfather had been threatened. With the thefts, he claimed he was just an occasional spare for lifting and carrying. And then he told me the story of his relationship with Sean, how he'd first been picked up, how he'd been dazzled by Sean and become infatuated by him -- then Sean had got bored with him.

Kyle started yawning so we had a beer and sat together in front of the TV. He put his arm round me, like brother and sister. When we heard Mel coming in, we jumped apart.

Later, in bed, I thought about Kyle, sleeping on the sofa outside. When I first knew him, I thought he and I might really get together. We'd had some fun, which he might have seen as something more than that. But I needed a much firmer base than Kyle or no base at all. Tonight, had I been too ready to trust him? Obviously he wanted my approval, but what would he do if Sean smiled at him again? He seemed so easily led. So should I be the one to lead him? I could easily have opened my bedroom door. Thank God I didn't.

And what about Tariq? Jill told me he was brought up as a Muslim. I thought that gay stuff was taboo for Muslims. So had Sean triggered his depression? And what could I do about that? I could at least show the hand of friendship to Tariq, see if he wanted to talk with me?

I couldn't ask Jill if she is happy with this idea. She would ask 'why?' I couldn't say because Tariq has passed on your passwords to Sean and by the way there's something happened between them. No, I had to approach Tariq privately....

30

The Africa-Read-Write website was by now well established in my style. Every two or three weeks Marion came to the Gallery and we did some updating. Jill often was elsewhere as Tariq was up and down. On one occasion, at the end of our session, Marion turned to me and passed me a printout.

'Sadie, I want to ask your advice. Yesterday I got this email. I want to know what you make of it.'

I read,

> *PRIVATE AND CONFIDENTIAL*
> *to Miss Marion Beckford,*
> *14a Parke Crescent, Brent Cross, London*
> *from Sinclair and Warton,*
> *Security Consultants,*
> *57 Gowell Walk, London E2 3SD*
>
> *Dear Miss Beckford,*
> *Sinclair and Warton are security consultants for your bank and we are writing you on their behalf. We understand that you hold an account with them, sort code 20-76-99, account number 04064147.*
>
> *We believe that you have a professional relationship with Ms Jill Carruthers in relation to the charity Africa ARW. We understand that Ms Carruthers has made substantial contributions to the charity.*

As I read the letter, my mind froze up and my throat constricted.

Marion said, 'Well? What's your reaction? You know Jill at least as well as I do ...'

'I ... I'm shocked. I don't know what to believe ... just let me read it again.' My voice was shaking -- my hands were shaking -- I could hardly read.

This was awful. And how I should react to Marion? That was critical. If I admitted knowledge, I would be part of this 'irregularity' -- a criminal. If I denied knowledge, what would happen? What would Marion do?

I had to prevent a catastrophe. It was the girls, the young women of Kembazi who would suffer…

Suddenly Marion placed her hand on my shaking hand.

'You're shocked -- I was when I first read this -- you obviously didn't know about it either....'

I breathed again.....my panic receded. I didn't want to hurt her so I gently moved back from her so that we could face each other..

I tried to speak calmly, 'You're right. I'm shocked. I really am. What does 'an irregularity' mean? It's so vague; it could be anything.'

'Yes but it says criminal proceedings, so there's something illegal, like theft or fraud or drug dealing. I can't have the charity linked with anything like that. It would destroy us.'

'Yes, that's obvious...'

'More than half of our funds come from Jill. This is terrible, but a scandal would put the other half at risk.'

'Yes it is terrible...'

Marion was becoming upset. 'How could she do this? I didn't suspect for an instant that she wasn't genuine, though I never really was comfortable with her life style. And her husband or partner or whatever he is -- he's so difficult. Then there's little Harry....oh dear me..'

Then to my surprise, Marion started sobbing. I took her hand and patted her gently to comfort her and found my hand grasped tightly by both of Marion's.

'Thank you Sadie, thank you. You're such a comfort.....'

As we sat hunched together, Marion sobbing and squeezing my hand, I was beginning to think that there was something odd about this letter. Why from this unknown security consultant and not from the bank? Why no further contact? Could this be another Sean trick? I needed to check up on this Sinclair and Warton, but I had to stop Marion from...what? Contacting the police? Her solicitor?

'Oh Sadie – sorry. I'm not often like this but I'm so shocked and saddened. I've got to talk to Jill, to challenge her. Sadie, you must come with me. It's not the sort of thing I want to do alone. I know I do most things alone, but if there really is criminality, then her words and her reactions are evidence. And it's always better to have a second person there. I'm right, aren't I?'

'Yes, yes. You're right. But we need to be careful. I'm suspicious about this letter. I'm wondering if it's genuine.'

'Oh it's genuine alright. They've got my address and my bank details. And why would anyone write such a letter if it wasn't genuine. It's obviously genuine, Sadie.'

'It's just a suspicion. It wouldn't be so difficult for someone to get hold of your bank details, especially if you do online banking. And there's loads of people who think that overseas aid is barmy. I don't know what Jill would do with her money if it wasn't for the charity, but I can imagine that some of her family members think she's mad, her brother for a start. Look Marion, I really want to check out this Sinclair and Warton firm, before doing anything else. It'll just take an hour or two.'

'I'm certain this letter is genuine.'

'Right, but a couple of hours delay is not going to make any difference, is it? Look, the letter was emailed yesterday, so an extra couple of hours is nothing.'

'Well, I suppose not.'

'It's something we need to know before approaching Jill.'

'Sadie, I'm not certain about approaching Jill now. I've changed my mind. The police or the ARW solicitor surely are the people to contact...'

'You're right. If this letter is genuine, then we'll want to know about the sources of her money. If this firm seems dodgy, then we're in an entirely different situation, where someone is trying to influence you by tarnishing Jill's reputation. We need to know which, don't we?'

'Alright. A few hours, but I'm sure you're wrong..'

'Can I keep hold of this printout, so I get the details right?'

'Well I suppose so. But don't show it to anyone else, will you...'

When I got home, the first thing I did was to look up the security firm Sinclair and Warton on the web. There was no website. There was no Gowell Walk. There was no such firm . Next I rang Jill and quickly explained to her what was going on. She was terrified by the news of the letter but calmed down when she learned that it was a fake. It was still frightening.

Next I scanned the email and sent the image to Jill. We spoke again on the phone when she'd read the letter and agreed how we were to react when Marion presented it to her. After that, I rang Marion and told her that the letter was a fake. She agreed to my suggestion that we would present the letter to Jill and see how she reacted.

I felt a heel because Marion trusted me. I knew that I was deep into the mire anyway and that if the sources of Jill's funding became known, I would be culpable. But the situation of Suzan, Olivette and their friends, was so much more dreadful that it strengthened my determination to do all I could to prevent any revelations. And if the letter came from Sean, then somehow or other, Sean had to be dealt with, whatever that might mean. I would think about that later.

Marion picked me up from the flat and we drove

together to the gallery, where Jill was waiting for us in the back office. Jill put on a good show of interest in the website and we touched on plans for the future. Tariq was rather better so that Jill was almost in full operation again. As far as Marion knew, Jill was completely ignorant of the letter and its contents. I just prayed that her acting would be good enough.

When we had finished the initial chatting, Marion took out a printout of the letter and placed it before Jill.

With a quavering voice, she said, 'Jill, you need to have a look at this e-mail. I've just been sent it.'

'OK -- what's this one about?'

Jill scanned through the record and gasped in indignation. 'My God, this is ridiculous. Some irregularity? Criminal proceedings? But the money comes from our family trust, from my Grandfather's business. You both know this. This is horrific -- and criminal. This letter is libellous. You don't believe any of this nonsense do you, Marion?'

'Well -- no, of course not. In any case Sadie has done some research and found that this Sinclair and Warton don't actually exist. Even the address doesn't exist. Someone is out to damage your reputation. Jill, I'm not sure what we ought to do about it. At first I was going to go straight to our ARW solicitor but now I'm not sure. I mean this letter is criminal, isn't it? This is a police matter.'

Jill stood up and paced backwards and forwards clutching the letter. 'Yes, yes, it is, but I'm pretty sure I know who wrote it. It's a family member. It's just the sort of trick he'd get up to. He's dead against anything to do with Africa.'

I said, 'Surely it's not a good idea to get the police involved if we can avoid it. It would be very difficult to keep the thing away from the media and that could mean gutter press rubbish about family rows. They would try to interview both of you. There'd be photos all over the place, twitter, the web. It would never end.'

Marion groaned. 'We cannot have that sort of thing, absolutely not. The good reputation of the charity is one of its strengths and one I have to defend. We can't allow any hint of scandal.'

Jill nodded. 'You're absolutely right Marion. No police, no solicitor. I need to deal with this. Can I keep the letter?'

'Yes of course you can. It's an e-mail anyway, but I won't do anything with it, least not without consulting you first. I mean if you can deal with it within the family and make sure no more of this sort of nonsense takes place, well, I couldn't ask for more. What do you think Sadie?'

'You're right. I agree with you completely. I mean the central point is getting these girls into education and any scandal linked with the charity is an obstacle to that, so if Jill can handle it, that would be perfect.'

Marion eventually left so Jill and I were able to consider what to do.

She was furious. 'It's Sean. It's far too clever for Baz or Kyle. It's got to be Sean. He's trying to cut off the ARW link, but he doesn't seem to realise that if Marion made a stir, it would be the end of the whole project, which is now paying him so well....'

'So what can we do?'

'My first reaction is – I'm not sure. I want to sleep on it. If we challenged him, he'd just deny it. But I want to let him we know about his silly trick and we see straight through it.'

31

I had invited Tariq to meet me in the same pub as we had used after the threatening call to my Grandfather. I sat down in exactly the same snug as we had used last time. He was a few minutes late. I wasn't sure what condition he'd be in but when he appeared, he looked neither manic nor drugged up, fairly normal in fact. This time I got a drink for him.

'Thanks Sadie, but I don't get why Jill hadn't to know we're meeting. I mean what's going on? People will talk if they see us. Know what I mean?'

'Look, is it likely there's anybody here that knows us? In any case this isn't about you and me, it's about you and Sean.'

He looked hard at me. 'Me and Sean? What do you mean? What are you on about?'

I hesitated, suddenly unsure whether I was going to achieve anything except more hurt.

'I'm just trying to understand Sean better – and you've worked with him for a bit…'

'Well, I dislike the guy. I told you that. I don't trust him, I try to keep out of his way…'

'But doesn't he massage you, your back?'

He stared at me. 'Who the hell told you that?'

I didn't want to mention Eva. 'Sean might have. I can't remember'

'So what? He trained as a masseur. I used to pay him to sort out my back. That's all finished.'

'Tariq, I've got the feeling that things got more complicated than a back massage -- and that, well, one thing leads to another…'

He bridled. 'What the hell does that mean? Do

you mean my illness? Because if you are, that's got nothing to do with Sean. How could it? And it's none of your business Sadie. Where do you get this rubbish from anyway?'

'I'm just remembering what you said before you rushed out. When Sean and the others brought the painting.'

'I wasn't well that day. What did I say anyway?'

'You said -- you disgusting pervert.'

He twisted his mouth and stared at me. 'Well he is, but that's nothing to do with me. So who's been talking? It's that Kyle isn't it?'

I tried to look neutral but failed.

He became very intense. 'I knew it. As soon as you started about me and Sean, I knew that someone's been getting at you. You know what? Kyle's a little creep -- and he's nasty with it. There's nothing between Sean and me. I've got a bad back; he trained as a masseur. He gives me a massage when things get bad. And that's it, except in Kyle's imagination. He's jealous and he's a stupid little prick.'

This was all said with such fervour that I was sceptical. I decided on a different tack, to see if I could bargain with him.

'Right. I understand.'

'And you believe me, Sadie, don't you?'

'Yes. Of course.'

'Right. Are we finished?'

'No, I just want to tell you about something, an experience I had with Sean a few weeks ago.'

'You? What was that?'

'I wanted to know how he put the web site together so I went over to his place. Kyle was out so there was only the two of us. We were sitting quite close and well -- physically he's, you know, attractive. Suddenly, without meaning to, I don't know what came over me, something happened. I was horrified by myself, but it happened. Then I was sick in the loo, not that he seemed to even notice that. All he said was -- well, he was very rude. He humiliated me. It was awful.'

'Oh Sadie, that's – that's – terrible. You're not pregnant, are you?'

'No, we didn't go that far...'

'Are you saying you gave him a......you know?'

'Something like that. Then he told Kyle -- and Kyle let me know that.'

I closed my eyes and tried not to cry. But the other part of me waited to see if Tariq would take the bait.

'They both mucked you about. They're a pair of bastards. Sadie, you didn't need to tell me that. I won't tell Jill. I promise you. But why did you tell me? It's none of my business...'

'Because Sean mucked you about as well. We've been in a similar situation. He uses people like you and me......'

He looked down, shaken and silent.

'Tariq, it's your turn to tell me something now, which I sort of know anyway.....'

He swallowed hard and stared at me.

'You trust me, Tariq, don't you?'

'Sure -- yes, definitely....but Sadie, this is too scary for me....'

'I know that. I know that you're a Muslim, Tariq.'

Tariq glared at me. 'I'm not gay -- right!'

'I know that. But something happened ...'

He looked down at the table and kept silent.

'And that something has -- put you in his power.

You didn't want it to happen. It just happened. Like with me.'

Tariq remained in the same position. He was not contradicting me. I waited. He said nothing.

I waited and waited, then said, 'We have to do something about it Tariq. We can't let this guy mess up our lives.'

He turned towards me and I saw tears of desperation. 'Don't you think I've said that to myself a thousand times? Sadie, he said he took photos of me -- and him. If they got out, I'd kill myself. '

'Oh Tariq -- no. Have you seen these photos?' He shook his head.

'Did you see him taking them?'

'He might have been lying about them but I can't take any risks. What can we do? He's got all the power. We can't use the law. If he even blabs about me, I'm done for -- me and my parents. I couldn't do that to them; they'd be forced out of their community. And if he blabs about the paintings, we'll all go to prison...except him that is. He'll just vanish.'

'We've got to do something. We can't just let him have his way and make those African girls suffer, take away their futures. We can't just sit here and accept that. So what can we do? Should we talk to Jill? Would she have any ideas?'

'Oh no. We definitely can't involve Jill. I forbid it. I can't bear for her to know anything about this. And in any case, you know her. She's hot tempered and sometimes she -- explodes. No, that's impossible.'

'I know what I want to do. I want to take revenge for what he did to my Grandfather...'

Tariq turned away from me and lowered his head right down on to the table.

'What's wrong? Tariq -- stop it...'

He put his head down and started knocking his forehead on the table. I got hold of his head and held it up to stop him, then put my arms around him. He was sobbing.

When he'd calmed down, he sat up and whispered into my ear, 'It was me threatened your Grandfather. I'm so sorry Sadie. He made me do it. He said he'd tell Jill and my parents...'

I went rigid. 'My God Tariq. I can't believe it...'

He whispered, 'Please, please forgive me. I was in a terrible state then...'

I stayed cool but had to know. 'There was sex between you?'

He nodded.

'And he threatened to tell your family...'

'Yes. People get stoned where my parents come from...I couldn't let them know -- and the shame of it. I was desperate.'

'So whatever he told you to do, you did.....'

Tears were streaming down his face. '....I'm so so ashamed.'

I looked at him. 'He ought to be kneecapped.'

'Oh, if only we could. I want to do it. Only thing is he'd still be alive. I've thought about this a lot and there's only one option. You see that, don't you? Do you agree?'

'What?' I stared at him. 'Murder? I'm not murdering anyone, if that's what you mean....'

'But I've gone round this a thousand times. It's the only way....'

'We can't do that Tariq. I'll have to think. There must be other ways -- something like bribing him to go away.'

'He'd just take the money and come back for more....'

We went round this loop a few times then Tariq became very tired. So we agreed to part and see if we could think up some other way of stopping Sean from doing any more damage.

'Sorry, it hits me like this sometimes, tiredness…'

'Do you need help to get home?'

'I'm not that bad. Do you mind if I go out first? Looks less -- you know.'

'That's fine. Text me if you have any ideas…'

And off he went. As if loads of folk hadn't noticed this mixed race couple in animated discussion…

Then nothing happened for a while. I had no further contact with Tariq about how to handle the Sean situation. We saw each other now and then. He had no answers and I was the same.

There was another theft in which I was not involved. It just seemed to be the old team, Julius, Jill, Sean and Tariq. As far as I know, Baz had been dropped; he was useless anyway. I think Kyle still occasionally filled in for Tariq but he was in fact living in the flat with Mel and I. I didn't see any point in telling Jill anything. I saw a lot of Kyle but kept my distance.

Presumably Sean got a bigger chunk of the takings. His skills were essential and if he was discarded by Julius and Jill, he said he'd trumpet their games to the press or the police. That would drag in Tariq and Kyle -- and me. I was involved, equally criminal. Oh God. This was getting too scary. Then I remembered that Jill was talking about me filling in for her in the next Africa trip, something I desperately wanted. This thought helped quell my fears.

32

An email from Dr Sophie Wilson arrived.

*Hi Sadie, if you have a spare hour sometime
please come round to our house again. My
Father has something very special he wants
to show you. I am sure you can guess what
that might be. If you are able to spare the time,
please call me and we will fix things up.*

Best Wishes
Sophie Wilson

As far as I knew, the Kandinsky had been
stolen for the father and was now hidden somewhere
in the house. After my initial visit, I had had no
contact, so this invitation was a surprise. Why should
Sophie Wilson want to see me again? They had the
painting so the matter was finished.

Part of me was holding on to the fiction that
I knew nothing of the thefts. This visit would put the
lie to that. I had seen the painting in the Simpson's
house and was involved in the theft. I had seen it
arrive at Julius's house and all the drama around that.
Dipping into the end of the story was very tempting
and could hardly incriminate me more. In any case
I had really liked Dr Sophie Wilson. I both liked her
style and rather admired what she was doing for her
father.

Ought I to seek Jill's opinion? No, there'd been
too much of that; I must decide for myself. So I called
Sophie Wilson and accepted her invitation.

Mel loaned me her small car and this time I drove right up the drive of the large Victorian house. The door was opened by the same smart self-possessed woman, but more informally and colourfully dressed.

'I'm so pleased you could come.' Then she gave me a hug, which was unexpected.

It flashed through my mind; should she be my new role model, Jill's successor? A foolish idea. And what exactly was she seeing in me?

'Thanks so much for coming Sadie. My father's waiting upstairs. He's got something special to show you.'

She stopped me at the foot of the broad curving staircase and spoke quietly.

'I don't think I told you. He's had a stroke which has taken away most of his speech but apart from that he's mentally bright -- and he understands everything'.

She ushered me up the stairs and into a large room at the front of the house, more of a lounge than a bedroom. A tall bald-headed man was standing by the window. He was in a light suit and tie. Perhaps dressed up for my visit?

"Father, this is Sadie. Sadie, this is my father, Richard."

We shook hands then stood back. What next? I looked round the handsome high-ceilinged room, with a bed at the far end. The tall windows looked down over the lawn and garden. Around the room were tall full bookshelves and some blown-up family photos.

'What a beautiful room. Who are all these people?'

Richard hand-gestured to the photos but Sophie supplied the words, 'This is my brother and his family -- and here my sister, her sons and daughter and grandchild. I'm the only one who hasn't married.'

Richard gestured that she had him to look after and that he was very grateful. Then he indicated that I should sit in the central of three seats placed in the middle of the room. Sophie sat beside me. Still standing, Richard drew my attention to a poster reproduction on the wall ahead of us. It was one of the earlier Kandinsky paintings.

I guessed, 'Composition Ten?'

Richard held up nine fingers.

Sophie spoke for him, 'You were near. Not a very good print though. But watch this.'

Richard moved to the reproduction, pressed the same sort of lever as Walter had, swung back the Composition Ten print to reveal the real Composition Twelve painting, which glided forward by some hidden mechanism.

I suppose I still gasped, 'Wow -- that's marvellous'

'We thought you'd appreciate it.'

I got up close to it again, just as I had in Julius's flat. Now it was placed up at a better level. Richard and I beamed to each other in appreciation of this wonder in his bedroom. I shook him by the hand.

"He'll understand if you want to speak to him"

"Richard -- it's truly marvellous. What a glorious object to have in your own room.'

He placed his hand over his heart and gestured to his daughter who had conjured up this end-of-life gift.

After more nodding and beams, I said, 'And what a clever mechanism. I've seen these before but not with gliding out. It's so clever. So no one will see this unless one of you allows it?'

'No one will see it except you. You are the only person that we could trust to see it.'

'Well, I feel honoured.'

In response to a question from Sophie, I told them what I knew about Kandinsky and this series of paintings. This took a while as this painter had been my special project in my degree course, so I knew a good deal.

After a while, I suddenly realised that Richard was nodding off. Was I that boring?

Sophie nudged me and whispered, 'This is a time of day when my father always has a snooze. We'll just leave him quietly and get some coffee.'

Downstairs in the kitchen, the coffee and biscuits were ready, obviously planned in advance. We sat opposite each other.

'You must have been surprised when I invited you here again...'

'Well yes, to be honest, I was curious to know your motives, but I understand a little more now.'

'Good. Who can I show off my little achievement to? No one apart from you. And you are someone who can really appreciate the painting.'

'Yes, I see that.'

'The other reason was curiosity to meet you again. I'm probably going to sound patronising Sadie but when you visited me, you seemed so fresh and enthusiastic -- well, you still are. Then the people who followed you seemed a different breed altogether.'

'How do you mean?'

'Worldly, looking at the bottom line all the time – and some of them might be criminals.'

My heart sank. Was she trying to corner me in some way?

'That might be so. I try to stay on the side of the angels.'

'Sadie, I'm not criticizing you or your colleagues.

After all I'm tarred with the same brush, aren't I? My father had to have that painting. He's obsessed with it. That's irrational, even slightly mad. He's all I've got in the world, sad but there you are. The money was sitting there doing nothing, so what should I do? I haven't got him for long. I had to indulge him.'

'Right. I understand.'

So that was that. Confessional over. Would I have done the same for Walter? Probably not but then he tried to do it for himself.

But she wasn't finished. 'I feel I'm treading on eggshells here Sadie. There's something else I want to say.'

What now? Time for a quick exit before getting into what? A declaration of love?

She looked me in the eyes. 'Sadie, don't you feel that you're being used? You're the decent front end of a murky trade and I don't want you to get hurt.'

So that was it. Time for me to enter the confessional.

'I'm aware of the risks. I'd better explain why I'm involved.'

I went on to describe the ARW organisation, briefly about my trip to Africa, meeting the girls and the way in which their lives were being transformed. She was impressed and relieved to know that some of her money was going in that direction.

As I was leaving, she said, 'My father only has a few years left -- and then I have a Kandinsky that I can't sell. If I could, I would love the proceeds to go into your African charity.'

'That's great to hear but as you say, you can't sell. What will you do?'

'Whatever happens, I don't want my father's reputation scarred by charges of receiving stolen goods, or mine for that matter. Your colleague Sean said he will take the painting away and has a safe place to hide it. He says he'll try to sell it and refund whatever he makes. Of course I'm not confident that will happen. I suppose I'm reconciled to losing the money, however knowing that some of it has gone to this charity is excellent news. It makes me much more comfortable.'

We parted saying that we must keep in contact, but I doubted that we meant it, much though I liked Dr Sophie Wilson and her father.

I could not see Sean helping when her father died, except the theft had to be kept secret. Would Sean still be around then? What nasty games might he try?

33

Jill asked me if I was prepared to go along 'for the ride' on a time-critical job with Sean and Tariq. I didn't want to think about it as my mind was on preparing to go again to Africa. Kyle was away somewhere but Tariq was recovered enough to handle the trip. According to Jill, I was to go to 'keep them apart'. I felt nervous at the idea of them being together and I didn't want to be anywhere near Sean.

'Does this really need a third person?'

'I just need you to keep an eye on Tariq, to make sure there's no trouble between them'

'Why don't you go? I'll look after Harry for the day.'

'That's a great idea Sadie but I'm running a children's party for a friend who's ill. I've got to be there. I'm organising it.'

Sean was loathsome. Tariq was unstable; I'd seen that when the Kandinsky was brought to Julius. He hated Sean and was probably still under his control. How could I possibly agree to go with them?

'I couldn't do it Jill. I couldn't keep them apart if they went for one another. Remember how Tariq nearly attacked Sean when he brought the Kandinsky to your father's place.'

'That was awful, awful. I still haven't got out of Tariq what the hell was going on. He says he was backing up Julius...I'm pretty sure he hadn't taken his pills that day, but that doesn't really explain it. I've never seen him like that before. It scared me.'

'Well if Tariq acted like he did then, I couldn't do anything...'

'But they get on fine most of the time. I know Tariq snapped that time, but mostly they get along well enough. Sean even sorted out Tariq's back problem.'

Jill didn't know much about what was going on in her partner's head, and I certainly was not going to change that.

'Surely they can go some other time, when you or Kyle could go along, or Kyle could go instead of Tariq? And what about Baz?'

'You're joking! Look, I've been over this again and again. I didn't want to ask you but this is time critical. Sean has access next Sunday. It has to be next Sunday. And I'll make absolutely sure that Tariq has taken his pills.'

I looked down, was silent. Then she played her trump card.

'You do want to go to Africa again Sadie, don't you?'

I was slightly shocked that Jill would use this so blatantly. I knew I was being manipulated in a fairly ruthless way. At that point, to go again to Africa was my strongest wish..

I hesitated before giving in. 'Alright. I'll do it -- reluctantly'.

Sean and Tariq were going to disable some below-ground surveillance cables, to allow easy entry into a gallery in Birmingham. Jill had told me they had a purchaser for a Turner 'Storm at Sea' painting, which was one of the treasures in Birmingham's Ambrosini Gallery. I knew that this was not Turner's greatest, but it would be a coup to acquire it. By this stage I must have been thoroughly corrupted to think that. I say corrupted as if someone else was to blame…

Tariq picked me up and we drove round to where Sean would be waiting with a van. On the way Tariq had told me that he'd fixed things and I should ask no questions. My heart sank. He would say nothing more.

Then he pulled up and gave me a small packet and said, 'Put this in your pocket.'

'What is it?'

'They're small fireworks and some matches. When I tell you, take them out and light them.'

'But why? I don't get it...'

'Don't ask. Then you don't know.'

I swallowed hard. I took them. Tariq was in a tense state

Sean's van was much bigger than the Telecoms one he'd used at the Simpsons. This one had black and orange streaks across the back door. He was already in the driving seat.

He said, 'Come on Sadie. You sit in the middle.'

When I hesitated he said, 'It's OK. I'm on my best behaviour. But I can't speak for Tariq here. He's got wandering hands.'

Tariq said, 'Fuck off'.

I didn't want to be anywhere near Sean, but my task was to keep in between them, so I just climbed in. Fortunately there was plenty of space on the bench seat.

I was genuinely curious about Sean's methods, and I wanted to keep Tariq quiet, so I plunged into questions about the job we were on. Jill had told me that the gallery had CCTV security but it was remotely monitored from miles away.

'So how did you find out that they used this remote system?'

He glanced at me slyly. 'Hey nosy, am I supposed to spill all my secrets?'

'I'm interested, that's all. It's not every day I get the chance to watch a guy like you at work. I'm on a learning curve.'

'Like making a web site?'

I turned away and felt like slapping him.

He raised his hands off the wheel, briefly. 'Forget I said that! Alright, I'll tell you. I hacked into the museum admin server for a list of security guards. Then I got a police mate of mine to check out the list and found a little jewel called Tim; he's really a great big guy. Anyway, he's got a police record of thefts and the museum doesn't know a thing about it. He's married with three kids; he's having an affair and he's in debt. Well, there you have it, a gift to folk in our trade. '

'Clever. So how did you approach this Tim?'

'E-mails, then we met in a bar. All he needed was some cash and the threat of revealing all to the museum -- and a hint of trouble for his kids, just to cut off any idea he might have of double dealing. The guy was a walk-over. He produced keys, the code for the inner door keypad and loads of stuff about the firm managing their remote CCTV.'

Tariq remained silent and still. I could almost feel the hatred directed at Sean. So I worked on keeping Sean chatting about the projects. He seemed to be quite flattered by my interest, once he'd got over questioning my motives.

'That's clever. So what exactly are we going to do now?'

'Today? We're going to set up a device to cut

the fibre-optic link from the gallery into the CCTV
monitoring centre. The brilliant thing is that the cutting
device is triggered by a mobile. I'll send off a signal to
chop the cable just before we go in to lift the painting
in a few days.'

'So where are we going now? The gallery?'

'No way. We're going to the monitoring centre.
It's run by a firm called Q-Sure. They service a load
of different places in the city from a central base and
that's where we're headed. Clever eh?'

I nodded. Extremely clever.

'I hacked into the Q-Sure system -- and found the
routing maps for the fibre optics. It'll take them an age
to discover where they're cut. That'll give us hours to
lift the painting.'

When I ran out of chat, I switched on some music.
Nobody objected and we made good time up the
motorway to Birmingham. At the last service station
before Birmingham, Sean parked in a corner of the
commercial area, then dished out high-vis jackets,
hard hats, a mask and gloves for Tariq to conceal his
colour, some specs for me, a scarf to conceal his own
beard.

'Remember, keep your heads down. There's a
camera at the end of the road and offices opposite but
we'll be hidden by the van and the barriers I've got in
the back.'

Around 3pm, on that quiet Sunday, Sean drove
our white van up to the front of the anonymous
looking Q-Sure surveillance centre, a mile or two
away from the Ambrosini Gallery. Q-Sure was housed
in a very bland two storey building. He turned on to
the side road round the corner from the entrance and
parked carefully beside a rectangular metal cover at

the outer edge of the pavement. Opposite the Q-Sure building was a tall office block with a few lights on here and there, out-of-hours workers like us. The van was placed to conceal the area around the metal cover.

Sean and Tariq jumped out. They placed 'Road Works' signs out to contain the van and the metal cover. They'd obviously worked together on this sort of process. I followed them but I just observed, and kept my head down. Tariq got manhole keys and a trolley device out of the van, then used these to remove the metal cover. Sean switched on a head mounted torch and shone it down into the chamber. It was the size of perhaps four coffins standing on their end, with a metal ladder fixed down the side. The two of us peered over Sean's shoulder.

'Look -- see that big pipe. That's the cables coming out of the building, then they split. Some go that way under the road south-bound. The gallery feed must be in that other bundle north-bound. All neatly finished off. And there's a nice shelf there for my little friend to sit on, but I'll have to open it up a bit first.'

From a shoulder bag, Sean drew out a device which looked like a high-tech mouse trap. We huddled between the open chamber and the van, aware of the windows high up over the road.

'This little baby is costly. It's a cable snipper, triggered by a mobile. See the little guillotine. That's going to be forced on to this plate by the worm drive. The blade and the plate go around the north-bound cables to cut off the images from the gallery. This is gonna be easy....'

I asked a stupid question, 'Why not fix it to cut them all off?'

'Because, clever-clogs, if we only cut some, they'll be confused and they won't look in here for a lot longer, that's why. Now while I'm down there, make sure no one gets too near. If anyone asks, we're installing new telephone lines -- OK?'

He placed the cable snipper into my hands and said, 'I'll tell you when I'm ready for this.'

Sean clambered down into the chamber and started gouging out the space where the cable snipper was going to sit.

Tariq said very quietly to me, 'Get the fireworks out now and light them there downwind, so he can't see them'.

My heart sank. I froze...

Tariq took me by the shoulders, grabbed the cable snipper from me and hissed at me, 'Light the smoke bombs Sadie. On the ground there -- now!.'

I delved into the paper bag he'd given me and fished out two things like fireworks and a lighter. My hands were shaking as I set the two squat smoke bombs on the pavement, downwind of the chamber, struck a match and lit them one by one. After a few seconds, they belched dense brown smoke.

Tariq whispered, 'When I say NOW, kick them in...'

Tariq eased up the manhole cover on the trolley, then mouthed 'NOW'.

In a clumsy gesture I kicked one in. Then the other. Sean roared and put his hand on the hole rim to get out but Tariq wheeled the heavy metal cover over the hole, withdrew the trolley. He stamped on it to get it into place. Muffled roars came from below as Tariq turned the locking bolts to clamp the cover in place.

I was horrified and stood staring at the cover. His fingers? I couldn't think...

Tariq hissed at me, 'Collect the signs. Get them into the van. MOVE!'

I couldn't move. He threw everything into the back of the van then bundled me into the passenger seat.

He started the van. I was in shock, felt sick.

'That was awful. Oh God. Look, there's someone coming along the road. They'll hear him. What shall we do?'

'Nothing -- he'll be smoked out when they get to him. She's wearing earphones anyway.'

We drove off. I was holding my legs to stop my hands shaking, trying not to be sick. Tariq looked shattered but he held it together and drove slowly back to the motorway where we stopped at the first service station. He drove into the furthest corner of the parking area.

I started weeping. Tariq took my hand and stroked it to soothe me. I was wretched. He took me in his arms and held me for a few minutes. It took me a while to get control of myself again. Then endless questions welled up in my mind.

'What the hell do we say to Jill -- and Julius?'

'Nothing. Because nothing's happened.'

I turned to him in horror then realised what he was saying.

'I'm going to leave the van by his flat, dump the keys, as if nothing's happened, as if he drove the three of us back. We left him outside his flat, got into my car and that's all we know.'

'Then when he doesn't turn up?'

'He kept talking about vanishing so he's done it. We don't know anything. He could have gone anywhere. That's none of our business.'

'And the Africa project? Without him, that's going

to vanish as well -- the girls...'

'Julius and I can fill the gaps. We've learned lots
of stuff from him, enough to do the easy jobs....'

Not true -- this man on happy pills who'd just done
a murder. His arms still around me to comfort me.
What on earth was happening to me?

After a few minutes of silence cradled in Tariq's
arms, I sat up. We needed strong coffee but images
of only two people on the service station videos was
not a bright idea, so I went in with my hood up and got
three coffees from a machine. We sipped these, then
we hit the road back to London.

We travelled largely in silence. Tariq went into
a slump. He looked exhausted and it showed in his
driving. I took over at the next service station. I'd
never driven such a big vehicle. The power steering
was good and the gears normal, but slow. I just had to
watch the mirrors to keep an eye on the road position.
Driving seemed to clear my head and then I was
consumed with the thought of getting back to my new
friends in Africa.

As we got near London, Tariq started to recover.

I was worrying. 'Aren't the owners of this van
going to chase it up?'

'Someone always comes for it.'

'Well doesn't that bother you?'

'It's not a problem. He gets it from a Telecoms
contact of Julius's. Someone else in his control. I've
seen the guy before when he's brought a van round to
Sean's. He'll collect the van to cover his own back...'

'With our finger prints all over it, and the image of
two people in a van and the number plate on loads of
cameras...'

'There's three of us. Sean's in the back, crashing

out – look I'm turning to have a chat with him. You alright back there mate? Feeling healthy?'

'Cut it out Tariq. That's sick…'

'I know. Sadie, speed up – you're going to attract attention…'

It was true. I was slowing right down. There was a bunch of heavy lorries behind me. I was stressed.

He took over the driving again at the next service station. I parked among other vehicles to avoid any cameras. I had to go to the toilet but I went in alone, with my hood up. When I got back to the van, other fears were flooding into my mind.

'When are they going to find the body?'

'I don't know. It could be months or years.'

'What if someone needs an extra fibre next week?'

'It's a risk. We've just got to hope not.'

'What about if the smoke went back along the pipes into the building – and set off fire alarms?'

'Oh God Sadie – you're going to drive us both mad. I'm a bit mad already. You've got to stay sane…'

'After what I've seen today?'

He nodded. 'Yes. Look, I had to do it.'

'I know that. And it can't be undone. I know you were forced into it…'

'I had no choice. I'm sorry you got dragged in as well….'

'It's done now….'

We drove on in silence.

But my mind would not stop churning. 'When they find him – what then?'

'Sadie, stop it…'

'I can't. They'll find his mousetrap thing, so they'll

214

know what he's up to. They'll find the mobile that sets it off. Maybe his personal mobile, wallet – all sorts of ID…'

He patted his pocket, 'I've got the mousetrap here. You gave me it.'

'Once the police get into his mobile, his contacts, we're doomed. It's a time-bomb waiting to go off under our lives.'

'Sadie. STOP.'

'We'll all have to vanish. I'm going to Africa soon. I'll just have to stay there. And you three will have to go somewhere…'

'Yes but I can't tell Jill. I mean about what's happened today…I can't tell her why I needed to do that. Nobody knows except that perverted little creep – and you of course…..but I trust you.'

'Do you mean Kyle?'

'Yes, bloody Kyle. He knows…'

Without thinking I said, 'I can shut Kyle up.'

'How? You can't mean…'

'No Tariq. I'm not going to murder Kyle…'

'Right, just joking…'

'I don't think much of your jokes, not today. I know Kyle. I can make him keep silent about anything to do with you and Sean.'

'That would be good, very good. Silence – for ever…'

'For ever is a bit long but leave it with me….'

We were now close to Sean's. I was getting scared again. We parked the van next to Tariq's car.

I asked, 'What happens to the keys?'

'There's only the one. It'll go down a drain. Sean's pal will have a spare.'

'Won't he call on Sean for the key?'

'Sean's not at home and he's not answering his phone. So if he calls, he'll be out of luck. You ready?'

I nodded then said, 'Not really. What happens if a neighbour sees two people getting out of Sean's van and driving off?'

'We dropped Sean off somewhere, a takeaway or something. He'll be back later. Simple. None of their business anyway. Let's go.'

He got out. I got out with my hood well up. He locked the van door – and we got into his car and quietly drove off.

Tariq dropped me off at my flat. We raised a silent hand to each other, then he drove off. Neither Mel nor Kyle was in – to my relief. I had a hot drink then dropped into my bed, shattered.

34

Next day, after a bad sleep, I felt terrible. During the night, I found myself living through all the detail of the previous day, then looking at the news on my phone to see if smoke had activated an alarm at Q-Sure. I obsessively checked this out several times all day, but nothing.

In the gallery, Jill came in late and quizzed me about how we'd got on.

'Tariq told me about it. Sounds like it was calmer than I'd expected. You didn't have to struggle too much to keep them apart?'

'No. They were fairly well behaved, once we'd got started.'

'Oh? Was there a problem?'

'Nothing much. Just Sean couldn't resist making a snide comment and Tariq had to respond. But it was all very low-key and we just focussed on the task.'

'Great. Sean seemed to have calmed down and settled for the new deal, which I resent but he's got us trapped'.

'Right'.

'And I don't know where it will go next.'

On the following day, Jill was out of sorts, worried.

'Sean didn't turn up for a planning meeting yesterday and we can't contact him. You haven't heard from him at all, have you'.

I felt panicky but tried to speak normally. 'No, I keep out of his way, so there's no way I'm going to hear from him.' This seemed a gross understatement.

'It's so unlike him. If he can't turn up, he always

lets you know. And I get anxious about the guy anyway. He threatened to contact the press or worse, then vanish. I mean, has he vanished?'

I had to hide my fears. I knew that if the body was discovered, the results of a police investigation would be a catastrophe for the lives of Jill, Tariq, young Harry, Julius, Kyle and me. Then there was Marion – and my African friends.

I wished that Tariq had talked to me first, rather than just plunging in and dragging me behind him. I would never have gone along with the plan, which was why he hid it from me. I wished I knew what ID was on Sean's body -- and for that matter what was in his flat. I decided to talk to Kyle, to see what he knew. I also had to silence him about Sean and Tariq.

'Sadie, are you alright?' My thoughts had blanked Jill out.

'Yes, fine, just you know, thinking about what you said...'

'I know. It's very odd behaviour for him. I mean has he vanished or has he gone off for a break or something? And I'm due to go to Africa with Marion next week. I'm not sure what to do. Will you take my place if I drop out again?'

'Well, yes. Right. Of course.'

'I'll let you know. I've got to rush now, to see Julius, see if he knows anything...'

And off she went.

Before leaving the gallery, I did my usual check on the news and the Q-Sure website. There was nothing.

When I got back to the flat, I was in luck. Mel and her boyfriend were out and Kyle had a night off from his bar work. We got some food together then I tackled him.

'Jill was saying she couldn't get hold of Sean. Do you know what he's up to?'

'How would I know, now that I live here? He never told me anything anyway.'

'Have you still got a key for his flat?'

'He never asked for it back and I never offered. But I'm not going back there again, thank you very much.'

'I know it's only three days, but he always responds to texts, e-mails and stuff. What if he's collapsed or got some bad drugs. What if he's lying dead inside his flat?'

'Don't be daft Sadie. Mr Control Freak isn't going to end up like that.'

'Well I think you and I ought to go round to his flat and just check up nothing is wrong'.

'What's the point?'

'I'm going Kyle, just to check up. I'll go by myself if you won't come.'

'You're wasting your time Sadie'.

'Maybe, but I'm going...'

'I don't want you finding any bodies all alone, but if he turns up, you'll have to do the talking. Can you want that?'

'Fine, but I doubt if he'll turn up...'

'It'll be messy. He doesn't even know we're.... friends.'

As an accomplished liar, I said, 'I'll cope.'

We borrowed Mel's little car and went round to Sean's flat. As we approached, I dreaded seeing the Telecoms van where we had left it, but it had gone.

Kyle and I let ourselves into the fourth floor flat. Pretending to look for Sean was absurd. As we entered the living room, the first thing I saw was the laptop and large monitor, of sordid memory. But for Kyle, this must have been even weirder, for he had lived here and as far as I knew, loved here. Anyway we were not on a sentimental journey, we were simply checking that Sean was not in the flat, alive or dead. But of course I had a secret purpose.

'He's not here, Sadie. He's off on some jaunt. Let's go. I've had enough of this place anyway.'

'Just let's check around for any clues about what's going on with him.'

'I don't want to know.'

'Give me a minute, I won't be long.'

Kyle sat down and switched on the television. I'd already checked around the living room and found nothing so I went into the bedroom. There was a wallet on the bedside table but no phones. In the drawer beneath, I found passports, two of them. I slipped them all into my pocket; theft was nothing against what I'd done recently. I was certain that Sean would have his personal phone with him. I just hoped that nobody rang him while a curious stranger was passing by that manhole.

Kyle shouted, 'What are you doing in there? Can we go now?'

'Nothing. Just poking around. There's nothing here.'

On the way towards the door, I unplugged the laptop from the large monitor and took it.

'Hey, what are you doing? Why've you taken that?'

I couldn't tell him what might be on it -- Jill's emails, Tariq's photos. I just herded him out of the flat, partly to give myself a chance to think.

'I just want to inconvenience him a little, that's all.'

'He'll have everything backed up.'

We left the flat and by ill fortune walked into a neighbour coming upstairs. She was a middle-aged woman in flowery clothes, full of smiles.

'Kyle. I haven't seen you in ages. How are you?'

I could tell he was a bit confused about how to react, 'Oh hi, Cynthia. Fine -- fine thanks. Just er, you know -- checking the place out.'

I thought that as an actor, he would do better than that.

I stepped in. 'Sean's away for a bit and we said we'd check up on the flat now and then.'

'That's so kind of you both. If I notice anything I'll give you a call. I've still got your number, Kyle.'

'Have you, good. Thanks. I'm sure he'll be back soon.'

She looked down at the laptop in my hand and paused. 'Has he gone far?'

I had a stock answer that I had rehearsed in imaginary interviews with the police, 'He's in Dublin for a month or two, maybe longer. He's got a job there.'

Kyle laughed and said, 'He's forgotten his laptop. He's always forgetting things. We have to send it on to him.' So he could improvise after all. I could almost have hugged him.

'Dublin, it's a lovely city is Dublin. And of course Sean needs his computer. I suppose he could work anywhere.'

I said, 'Yes, he's a clever guy. Look we must press on now, get this sent off....'

Once we were out of the woman's hearing, Kyle asked, 'How do you know he's in Dublin? That's news to me.'

'Jill mentioned something. I might be wrong, it

might have been Edinburgh or somewhere. I just wanted to get away from that nosy woman. Do you know her well?'

'She's just a neighbour. Harmless enough though.'

When we got back to the flat, Kyle flicked through the TV channels and settled on another re-run of a silly comedy.

'Can you handle this?'

'Just about, but there's something I want to ask you first.'

'That sounds scary. What now?'

'Just keep to yourself that stuff about Sean and Tariq...'

Kyle turned to me in surprise. 'Well who am I going to tell? There's only you...'

'I mean I want a firm promise – a lifetime promise Kyle.'

'Talk about dramatic. We're not on the stage you know....'

'I know, but I'm serious...'

'Alright. I promise. Never to tell anyone. Right?'

'Kyle, this is really serious.'

'Is it? Alright, I promise to never tell anyone about Sean and Tariq. Is that good enough for you? Sometimes I don't know what you're on Sadie. Now can I watch this bloody programme, please?'

Later, when Mel and Justin were back, I went off to my room to see what was in the wallet. A few cards, a bit of cash, nothing much, but I took the cash. There was no point in wasting that. I could still hear my dead mother's voice -- Sadie, good girls never steal.

Of the passports, one was Sean's, the other had the same photo but a different name – one of his props for vanishing?

I suppose more personal stuff was all in the phone with him; I quaked at that thought. And on the laptop, which I had. I removed a hard disk then I scraped off all identification from the laptop and put it in a plastic bag. Next day, when I left the flat, I took all the items I'd taken from Sean's flat. The passports and wallet went down a large drain in a quiet cul-de-sac. The plastic bag went into the local rubbish collection skip. The hard disk went into the canal, where it sank with all its secrets.

Two days later, I was in the gallery as usual, playing around with the websites, when Jill came rushing in.

I said, 'Hi. Looks like you need a coffee?'

She looked worried. 'No, no. I need to talk to you. Let's go into the office.'

I followed her in and we sat down at the work table.

'Sean's vanished. Julius and I are desperate. He said that if things didn't go his way, he was going to shop us then vanish. He's gone, so now we're just waiting for something to happen. Sadie, we're going to have to get away for a bit, the three of us, and Julius if I can persuade him, which I can't. Tariq's brother's in Ottawa and Tariq's got a joint Canadian passport, so we'll go for a holiday there.'

'Right – so will you come back if everything stays quiet?'

'I'm not sure. They might come for us in Canada. We don't know. And Sadie, I have to think about you as well. I mean you're almost family. But first, can you go to Africa in my place again next week? I'm sure that'll be safe at least.'

'Well yes. I'd like to, but what if – the police or

anything? Do you think I ought to be worried?'

'Not as much as us. Remember you know nothing.'

My heart sank. I said to myself I know a great deal more than you do….

'But Jill, what's the point in going to Africa if Sean is….whatever…'

'I know what you mean. But he might come back. We just don't know. In any case, there's a fair chance ARW will survive at a lower level. Until we know anything for certain, we just have to hope for the best. You want to go, don't you?'

'Yes. I think so…'

'I think it'll be fine, honestly. Things might get complicated financially with Marion and everything. But we'll keep in contact by e-mail or text. And if things get really scary you can come to Canada as well. Tariq wouldn't mind and Harry would be thrilled.'

'But how would I know? I mean I'd be booked to come back with Marion as normal, wouldn't I? What would I say to her?'

'I'll let you know if it's not safe for you to come to the UK -- or Julius will.'

'But won't he be with you in Canada?'

'Well at present I can't persuade him to come. He says he'll just weather the storm, whatever comes.'

So that was it. The world was falling apart but I was off to Africa again, unless someone decided to open a manhole. I really had the jitters. The deceit, lies and now murder were all horrific, but somehow none of it really felt like my fault. It had all slowly accumulated. There had been lots of chances to say *stop*. Stop all of this. Get out. Live a sensible life. This must be like what it is to be criminal. I still

think of myself as being a decent person. Instead
I find that I have to lie more and more. I've been
knowingly involved in major art theft and I've been an
accomplice to murder. Liar, thief and murderer. Quite
a list....

Why didn't I feel traumatised by my situation? It
was as if these awful events had glided past me and
left me untouched. This is how criminals must feel.
None of it was really my fault.

I was beginning to become excited about going to
Africa again. If it wasn't safe for me to come back to
the UK, Jill or Julius would let me know. I was plunged
into confusion by this. How to plan? What about
money? What about Mel? What about Walter?

Mel was simple. I told her I might be away for a
bit. I handed the details of domestic bills to her, and
she was perfectly happy.

Walter, not so simple. If I was away for a while,
perhaps even weeks or months, would he even be
alive? I decided I'd have to tell him something about
the uncertainties of my future. He was my closest
family member and after all, it was the threatening
message on his phone that had triggered all this.
So two days before going back to Africa, I spent an
evening with him.

By mutual agreement, we had not discussed the
attempted purchase of the Bacon self-portrait again.
I knew that the photographic print was still in the
concealed chamber above the fireplace, because I
had checked it when Walter was in the bathroom. So
it was as Jill and Tariq had said. Everything about that
deal had been frozen.

'So you're off to Africa again -- in place of Jill?'

'Yes, she's planning a family holiday in Canada.

Tariq's got a brother there.'

'Sounds nice. And you're flying off with the delightful Marion? When my dear?'

'Wednesday. And I could be staying a bit longer this time?'

'Right. And is that good?'

'Grandfather -- I'm honestly not certain...'

'Not certain how long you'll be staying? Or not certain if it's good?'

'Both...'

'Oh. This sounds like the Julius-Jill business is going into free-fall? Everyone is running away. Or have I got it wrong?'

'I'm not certain but one of their guys has vanished and they think this is the time to stop anyway.'

'Vanished? With pots of cash I suppose......and meanwhile you go out to organise more schools? Is that sensible?'

'No, well, as far as I know, the charity has access to other funds and with luck, they'll keep the existing schools going. That's the hope anyway. But Marion doesn't know this yet.'

'That could be awkward. Jill will have to tell her before you two fly off.'

'That would be ideal, wouldn't it?'

'Essential I would have thought.'

I had the sinking feeling that I might be left carrying the message of doom to Marion.

'If I'm away for a while, Mel will look after things on the flat, pay the bills and everything. She's very reliable.'

'I'm sure that'll be fine. She's a good friend to have. Now what's the longest you might be away?'

'That's the trouble. I don't know, but I'm hoping to

be back with Marion on Sunday.'

I knew that Jill's fears were groundless as Sean was not going to blab to anyone, but my concern was if someone was to open up the chamber where he lay, I would rather be in Africa. I had sleepless nights thinking of the smoke from the bombs I had ignited, flowing along the pipes into the security building and setting off fire alarms.

'Well Sadie, it sounds like you're keeping some of this to yourself. You must have good reason.'

He was right. He knew me well.

'Grandfather, I guess I'm following your example there, just keeping a few secrets.'

'Touché.'

He looked at me quizzically.

'I promise I'll tell all when it's safe to do so.'

He patted his chest and said, 'Alright, but you haven't very long. Just remember that...'

'You keep saying that, but then I see the twinkle in your eyes...'

'Do you? That's nice....'

'I'll send you emails, keep you posted.'

'That's not the same thing as having you here...'

I came round behind his chair and kissed him on the top of his head.

'I know, but I'll be back. So you don't go anywhere. Right?'

'I'll try darling, not that it's in my control any more....'

And I left him, perhaps for the last time.

35

A few days later Marion and I were on the weekly plane to Kembazi. The journey out was the same as last time, almost familiar, but everything else had changed. Jill had met Marion and told her that her sources of funding were frozen for a while. As a consequence Marion launched a major moaning rant but I had learned how to contain this.

At the capital airport, during the wait for the internal flight, I picked up emails on my phone. There was an email from an 'anonymous' sender which I thought was a scam until I read the first line.

I've set up this temp e-mail. Things bad. Julius interviewed by police. He won't say anything. I'm scared.
Hockney painting with client -- she died. Relatives priced it & found it was stolen. Linked back to Julius. Sean was supposed to be checking.
We three to Tariq brother tomorrow. Hope they dont block our passports when we try to leave. Tariq is ill again.
Sadie, feel awful for getting you into this. You can come to us but stay in Kembazi for a few weeks to see what happens. I'll try to let you know. Is there anywhere else you can go? I don't think you should come back to UK for a bit.
Don't reply to this because they might be tracking you. Get another phone & a new email

So catastrophe was upon us. What the hell should I do now? I panicked; my head was in a total whirl.

A voice said, 'Sadie dear, what's wrong?'

Suddenly I was back in the airport lounge, facing Marion. It was catastrophe for her as well as for me.

'Oh -- nothing really. It's alright. My Grandfather's had another heart attack, a small one. I was thinking I should be there with him...'

She came over to sit by me and took my hand. Then I had to follow through on my silly lie. I escaped to the bathroom as soon as I could. I couldn't tell her the truth about what was likely to happen, the drying up of funds, the damaging publicity for Africa ARW. The charity would fold. Marion's life would be wrecked. And what about Suzan, Olivette and the others? I felt wretched.

Joseph, the head teacher, was waiting for us at the small airport of the second city and off we went on the bumpy ride to the school. He avoided personal matters with Marion. She explained to him in endless detail that funds were still decreasing, so this trip was about planning how to withdraw from some earlier commitments, including the construction of any new school.

Next day, when we got to work, I was Marion's PA, and her pedantic fussiness washed over me. Taking notes and then writing them up fairly straightforward, except for the priorities for possible future expansion, which were now absurd dreams. Jill had told me that Sean's games had resulted in a ten percent reduction in funds, but now everything was likely to end. Even Joseph's job, his family house? I just played dumb about all of this.

I wanted to meet Suzan and Olivette again. Later in the afternoon, Marion needed a rest and Joseph was busy with some office work so I went to the female dorm where several girls were washing their clothes. Suzan and Olivette were there. After some general chatter, the two of them said they had to show me the new vegetable garden. I was pleased as I thought this could be my last chance to be with my friends, as I thought them.

As soon as the three of us were alone, Suzan became quite challenging.

'Madam, I want to ask you a question.'

'Alright, what is that?'

'My cousin wants to go to school in Dalobi but we are hearing that the new school will not be built. Why not? Is this not what Madam Marion is coming here for?'

'Marion is doing her best with the funding that is available.'

'Madam Sadie, my cousin lives five miles from Dalobi and that is where she wants her education. Will this school be built?'

'I know it is bad news Suzan, but this is completely out of Marion's control. We depend on people giving their money. Sometimes we get enough to build a new school. Sometimes we only get enough to keep the current schools running. At the moment, people are not giving so much.'

'But why not? They are selfish. I know they are very rich because we have seem films showing all their wealth. They have big cars, big schools, big houses, everything big.'

'It's true. I'm sorry Suzan. We've let your cousin down -- it's wrong.'

I turned to her friend. 'What do you say about this, Olivette?'

'It is very unfair. Money should be spread out evenly around the world.'

'You're right. At the moment the opposite is happening. A few people are getting very rich and many people are getting much poorer. We must use our education to change that.'

Suzan said, 'I want to do that, but how?'

'You must get into politics and influence people to be fairer.'

'That is much easier if you are a man...'

'Maybe, but you can argue for a better world. I've just heard you do that..'

Olivette said, 'That's true, Suzan. You are the schools' best arguer. She sometimes makes the teachers angry with her. She'll be a good politician. President Suzan!'

This discussion left me feeling helpless. Life is such a lottery. How can you change anything when you can't even get the promised funding for a new school? And why should I have come out of this lottery so well, at least compared with these two? As for their cousin, I felt ashamed, but that is so pathetic set against lost life chances.

Jill was right. I was going to have to stay. But what about Mel and my Grandfather? I couldn't think about any of that, not yet. I decided to get through the next day before telling Marion that I had to stay. As usual we were only in Africa for three nights. I decided to tell her as late as possible.

In the evening, we had a meal with Joseph, Augusta and their family. We had a highly flavoured goat stew with rice, followed by cake and biscuits. Alpha again looked after the drinks. Then we played a local variation of 'I spy' which the children found very hilarious. After that we went through plans for the return journey leaving early in the jeep, then Marion and I made for our sleeping quarters. At last I got her on her own. It was a beautiful moonlit evening; it was cool and the insects weren't bad. She agreed to a short walk along the road towards the village.

'What a clever idea on our last night. Good for the digestion too. I really don't want to go back at all, but there's a mountain of stuff to do when we get back....'

We walked in step along the wide track, amid the loud chorus of insects.

I braced myself and plunged in. 'Marion, there's something I need to tell you. I'm going to stay here for a while.'

'Stay here? At the school? But the flights are booked Sadie. We can't just change them. In any case, as I said I've got meetings later this week.'

'No -- I want *you* to go back. I want a bit of time here. I'll probably help with the teaching...'

'Sadie dear, that's a lovely idea but it's quite impossible. You wouldn't be safe on your own... I mean, we must be sensible.'

I stopped and turned to her. 'Marion, I mean it. I'm staying. Probably not for long. I'm perfectly capable of looking after myself.'

'I'm sure you are, back home, but here? I've seen the men looking at you. You wouldn't be safe. A young white woman on her own? Anyway, what about your Grandfather? Don't you need to look after him, poor man?'

I was trapped by my lie. 'I know, but it isn't so serious this time, just a small attack, more like an echo of the previous one.'

We stood on the jungle track, batting away the insects.

I was beginning to feel desperate. 'Marion, I am serious about not returning yet.'

'I can tell that Sadie, But you're here working with ARW and I'm the designated ARW officer. You're working under me. I am saying this to you. You are not going to stay here by yourself.'

We stood facing each other. I was going to have to say more. She was going to find out anyway when she was back in the UK. I was sort of stunned and hadn't realised how strongly she would object. I couldn't tell her the whole story...

After a few moments of silence, Marion said, 'I'll take that as a yes, that you accept my authority. You'll be travelling back with me and we'll have no more of this nonsense, thank you very much.'

'No Marion, I won't be coming. Really. You'll be returning to Britain with an empty seat beside you. This is nothing personal, believe me. Look, something's happened while we've been away. Jill's in serious trouble. I don't know any details but I want to stay here for a while, just to sort things out in my head, if you like.'

'I don't understand that. How do you know Jill is in serious trouble. What sort of trouble? And why do you need to stay here? In any case you can *always* sort things out in your head. That's precisely why I agreed to you coming to assist me in the first place.'

She was right of course. I gave her another long silence, just to show that I needed time to think.

'It's something financial, I mean Jill's problem. That's all I know...'

More silence, then she said, 'Has it got something to do with that letter? The bank security thing, family blackmail or something? It has, hasn't it?'

'I honestly don't know. It might be that there was something in that...'

'But you checked it out. It was fake.'

'Yes, yes I did, but I think there's some sort of blackmail going on, something like that.'

'Blackmail? That's what Jill said, but within her family. Was it her brother? Well if there's still anything of that sort going on, there's a risk of ARW being damaged. We live on our reputation. I am going to have to go back. And you're coming with me Sadie. I need your support in this. You owe me that at least!'

I gave her another long pause and gritted myself. 'Marion, I do owe you a lot and I'm grateful to you, but I'm not coming with you. You have to go to back to the UK. I'm not coming with you.'

I quickly turned away from her and walked back to our sleeping quarters. I couldn't tell her anything else about the Jill business and we couldn't just go on and on saying the same things to each other. I got into my room and jammed a chair against the door, turned the light off and got into bed, fully clothed.

After a few minutes, I heard her coming into the rest house. She came straight up to my door and knocked. I lay in bed and kept completely silent.

She said, 'That was very rude of you, walking away like that. We haven't finished our discussion.'

After a further long pause, she tried to open my door, and found she could not. She waited, knocked again and again, then went to her room.

After I thought she'd settled down, I wrote a note
for her. It said,

> *Dear Marion, sorry to ask you to do this but
> I depend on you. When you get back, will you
> please ring my friend Mel at the flat – you have
> the number – and say to her that I can't return at
> present but that I am safe and well, but please
> don't try to contact me. Also please ask her to
> pass the same message to my Grandfather and
> Kyle.*
>
> *Thank you for your help Marion.*
> *Best wishes and love*
> *Sadie*

I sealed it up then I tiptoed out and made for
Joseph's house. I couldn't stay without his agreement.
Through the insect mesh, I could see that he and his
wife were reading. I knocked on their door.

My arrival was a surprise for them both, and my
request even more so. I just prayed that they would
go along with my plan.

'It'll only be for a few weeks at most and I'd love to
teach your pupils.'

'I think they would appreciate that very much. But
I have a problem. We have no spare funds, so I can't
pay you.'

'Joseph, I don't need paying, honestly. I've got
money. And I can get more sent out if necessary.'

I was uncertain that this was true. I didn't know
what was going on in the UK with the police. They
might have access to my phone and bank records by
now, but I had to persuade Joseph to let me stay.

Joseph's wife said, 'if you're just here for a
few weeks, you won't need any money. Joseph,

surely Sadie can eat with us. The children would be thrilled...'

So it was arranged but for one more hurdle.

'One problem is that Marion is against me staying. She wants me to travel back with her tomorrow. We had a row about it earlier.'

Joseph stared at me in surprise. 'But if Marion is against you staying, it is very difficult for me to oppose her.'

'I know that Joseph. I don't work for Marion. I simply came out to assist her with her work here. My job is finished now and I'm a free agent.'

'Well I know that women have different ways in your country. Let me ask you this -- what if Marion refuses to leave without you?'

'She has to go back to the UK. She's got a full schedule later on this week. Joseph, I won't be around when you leave. I'm going to be well away from the school. Nobody will know where I am so you can't do anything about it. You're not going to lock me in my room and then drag me into your jeep, are you?'

His wife laughed and said, 'Of course he's not. He's a good kind man, most of the time.'

'I try to be but this is a unique situation you're presenting us with, a sort of moral dilemma.'

'I know that and I'm so grateful to both of you. One last thing Joseph, will you please pass this envelope to Marion once you are on the way? It's just asking her to pass on a message to a friend once she is in the UK, so people know I'm safe.'

I knew exactly what time Marion would have to leave. Shortly after dawn, I set off walking away from the school, along a bush track. It was quite narrow. I had jeans on and was on the watch for snakes and biting insects. It was quite scary. Trailing foliage kept hooking my clothes, holding me back. This gave me the jitters but more was the feeling that I was deliberately hiding away from Marion and cutting myself off from my booked flights. And from my poor Grandfather, the smoke bombs, the body. It was all awful.

I really wanted a good cry but plodded on, away from the school compound, then I thought I heard something behind me. I stopped, it stopped. I started. It was still there. Oh God, what now? You've been a bloody fool again. Some wild animal? Or a man?

I went around a bend, waited, then rushed back. To my amazement it was Suzan and a girl I didn't know.

'Madam, sorry to be following you, but it is not safe for you to be out by yourself.'

Tears came to my eyes. I was thrilled and relieved to see them. That they should show such care was wonderful.

'Madam, are you angry with us for following you?'

'No, not at all. But how did you know I was out here?'

'A boy saw you, one of the pupils. He was up early. He came to call me that you were on this path.'

'Oh thank you, thank you. I'm so grateful. I was being a bit silly, wasn't I?' They nodded in agreement.

'You see I'm going to stay here with you all and do some teaching.'

They were so pleased with my news that I started crying. I knew that they liked me a lot and it was rather wonderful to just be staying with them, away from the Marion complexities, away from Jill and Tariq.

I checked my watch and to their surprise said,

'Can we keep walking for another few minutes?'

'But why Madam?'

'.....because I would find it very hard to say goodbye to Madam Marion...'

The teaching went fine, delightful even. I was working with pupils younger than Suzan and Olivette. Their English was at starter level but we had great fun and they really worked hard for me.

I had to hold back approaches from a couple of male staff members -- but Joseph and his wife were very protective. Suzan and Olivette were never short of advice.

To my relief I was able to get cash out of the UK. I had to go to the local town to do this. The UK police appeared to take no interest in me. After a week or two I bought a new SIM card and started using my mobile on the local network. I set up a new email account and used it to write to Jill, telling her about my current life.

Jill and her family were staying in Canada. Julius was in custody awaiting trial for art thefts.

I got into contact again with my aunt and uncle in South Africa – and let them know where I was. They asked me to visit them if possible and said if I wanted to stay for a while, they would fix up some work for me. That was a lifeline. I found that I couldn't stay at the AWR school in Kembazi for long, though I did enjoy being there. The pupils were great and so grateful for my help, and I was surrounded by warmth and friendship. But even though thousands of miles away, I was plagued by fear of that manhole cover being opened. The images of what was down there terrorized my dreams so I often slept badly then faced most mornings in discomfort.

I was homesick for the UK. The sense of isolation began to weigh me down, also I was getting pestered. If I went into the local town, I was followed, stared at, brushed against. It was all fairly good-natured, boring stuff but it oppressed me. Marion had warned me.

When my South Africa aunt and uncle offered an escape I grabbed it, while dreaming all the time of going home to Britain. On my arrival in S.A., my aunt and uncle soon realized that I was in trouble, that I was avoiding returning to Britain. I had to devise a failed romance based around a fictionalised version of Kyle. I found this alarmingly simple as I had become a competent and convincing liar but it became painful, this fictional life I might have had, so I persuaded my relatives that it was all too painful to talk about. My kind aunt was so understanding, I felt a heel.

36

Now it's four years since I left Kembazi. Cape Town is reasonably safe and congenial but it's not where I want to be. I'm still marooned in a foreign country. I use email and text a lot to ease the pain of separation.

I'm working in a private school teaching Art and English, largely to foreigners. I have my own small flat, my aunt and uncle are nearby – and I have made a few friends and one very close friend, Thomas.

Mel and I message each other most weeks. Her boyfriend Justin has moved into the flat and they pay rent to Walter. Kyle and I are out of contact; he is doing bar work somewhere.

Jill keeps me briefed. She feels guilty about me, which I do nothing to discourage. Julius is in prison and there's probably still a search warrant out for Sean. Julius has shouldered the blame for two art thefts and has successfully shielded Jill and Tariq. That sounds incredibly generous, but he adores his daughter.

Tariq is well again and is working with his brother in a car rental business. Harry, now eight, is very athletic and quite tall. Jill has sent photos and Harry looks quite different. Jill herself has moved back into the art gallery and consultancy world in Canada, and is keeping on the straight and narrow as far as I can tell.

Marion and Jill managed to isolate Africa ARW from scandal, but its income was more than halved overnight. About two years ago, Jill used her persuasive powers on a similar Canadian charity, and the two have now merged, so that the running costs of the current AWR schools are covered. This is wonderful news.

I get regular emails from Walter. Time is running out and he wants to see me again. I can't deny him that.

I followed the UK news on the web, obsessively, waiting for Sean to be found and identified, then after more than four years in South Africa, I got the news from Jill. Tariq may have told her what he'd done, what we'd done I should say….

She sent this article to me. She just said – Tariq and I think you'll be interested in this,

POSSIBLE HUMAN REMAINS
FOUND IN INSPECTION CHAMBER
While conducting an inspection, security engineers found deposits which may be human remains in an access chamber beneath a Birmingham pavement. It is not certain that the deposits are definitely human because of the destructive action of rats. Police say that if the remains are human, DNA testing may reveal an identity. Also found were the badly chewed remains of two mobile phones.

When I read this, my spirits soared. Thanks to the rats, I was apparently free of the haunting fear of the discovery of my crime. Then I crashed at the thought of the DNA being linked with Sean, but why would the police have his DNA on file?

I reckon I can return to the UK, to Walter's flat, reasonably safely. I'm in a relationship with Thomas, a lovely local guy. He's at uni studying Engineering, with a year to go. He's clever and good natured.

I'm not pregnant, so what happens now? When I started writing this, I had the fanciful idea that it was for my unborn children. Thomas and I could have beautiful children, but so far in my life, beauty has meant danger. There'll be no children until I'm certain that we're both ready and safe.

I have not yet told Thomas that I'm thinking about returning home. Do I take Thomas with me to the UK, if he'll come, or leave him here in his homeland? Or split our lives between two homelands? That's what I have to think out now.

I am developing my plans for the future. I am still very determined to support the education of girls in Africa and hope that over the years, the moral balance can move towards positive and my conscience be eased. I want to feel that my sins can be washed away by getting more girls into education without breaking any laws.

Jill feels the same. She now runs a couple of galleries in Ottawa. ARW is chugging along under Marion, keeping the existing schools running but she would welcome a boost.

My new idea is to persuade wealthy investors in art, to give ten percent of their profits to ARW when they sell. I think I could persuade the likes of John Simpson (from whom the Kandinsky was stolen) to agree to this. It could become a fashionable act.

37

I am back in the UK now, without Thomas. The current idea is he'll join me when he has finished his course, but we'll see. Walter is on new pills and going strong. Justin is in the flat with Mel so I've moved into my old room in Walter's house. He is thrilled and is becoming interested in working out some viable finances for the new plan. The day after I got back, he was so happy, beaming with glee.

'Sit down. I've got something to show you…'

He got up, went to the concealed painting device, pulled the lever and swung the familiar portrait round to reveal -- the Bacon copy -- or was it? I jumped up to get a close look and was shocked.

'My God Walter. This is the real thing.'

'You're right. Isn't it fantastic?'

'But why is it here? How on earth did you get it?'

'Julius said I might as well have it. It was just sitting in the store behind your old gallery. He sent out an instruction from prison -- and this guy just brought it round, with no warning. He said, this is with compliments from Julius. Keep quiet about it.'

'Who? Who brought it?'

'He'd been here before. He brought the Bacon copy. We had quite a chat. He hung it for me in there. Some vegetable name, Kale perhaps?'

'It was Kyle.'

'Yes, that's it. Silly name. You know him.'

'I used to…'

Walter was looking healthy but still, I had to say, 'But surely you can't just keep it. It's stolen.'

Nobody knows about it so can't I just enjoy it?'

I was dismayed. I so wanted to make amends for the past but living in the same house as this Francis Bacon painting which had started my slide into sin, was an awful idea.

Something clicked in Walter's mind. 'Oh, you mean when I pop off?'

'I didn't mean that Grandfather, but it's a good question. The painting becomes my problem then, I suppose.'

'Not at all. Just wrap it up well and get Kyle to quietly leave it on the doorstep of wherever it came from. Julius will know.'

www.ingramcontent.com/pod-product-compliance
Lightning Source LLC
Chambersburg PA
CBHW070443120726
47910CB00003B/904